ABOUT THE AUTHOR

With over a million books in print, Pamela Britton likes to call herself the best-known author nobody's ever heard of. Of course, that changed thanks to a certain licensing agreement with that little racing organization known as NASCAR.

But before the glitz and glamour of NASCAR, Pamela wrote books that were frequently voted the best of the best by the *Detroit Free Press,* Barnes & Noble (two years in a row) and *RT Book Reviews.* She's won numerous awards, including a National Readers' Choice Award and a nomination for the Romance Writers of America's Golden Heart® Award.

When not writing books, Pamela is a reporter for a local newspaper. She's also a columnist for the *American Quarter Horse Journal.*

Books by Pamela Britton

HARLEQUIN AMERICAN ROMANCE

985—COWBOY LESSONS
1040—COWBOY TROUBLE
1122—COWBOY M.D.
1143—COWBOY VET
1166—COWGIRL'S CEO
1285—THE WRANGLER
1322—MARK: SECRET COWBOY
1373—RANCHER AN
1407—THE RANCHE
1453—A COWBOY'S

HARLEQUIN HQN

DANGEROUS CURVE
IN THE GROOVE
ON THE EDGE
TO THE LIMIT
TOTAL CONTROL
ON THE MOVE

This one's for one of the best barrel racers around. A person whose smile always lifts my spirits and who's so great at listening and offering words of encouragement I swear you're an angel on earth. You may have a bladder the size of an elephant, but your heart is even bigger and I want you to know that I appreciate you, Kelli Nichol.

Chapter One

"Well, well, well, if it isn't Saedra Robbins."

Saedra's whole body jerked at the sound of that voice, the piece of luggage she'd been in the middle of pulling out of her rental car momentarily forgotten.

She closed her eyes, blotting out the California mountains and pine-studded meadows that surrounded her.

Cabe Jensen. The fly in her soup. The splinter beneath her nail. The rock in her shoe. Too bad he would be her host for the next two weeks.

Taking a deep breath, she turned to face the man. "Cabe," she said with as pleasant a smile as she could muster.

He stood on the porch of his two-story Victorian home painted the color of an autumn forest—buttercup-yellow—his hands resting on the white railing. From nowhere came the thought that he looked like the quintessential master of the manor standing there, his tall, broad-shouldered frame the epitome of masculinity. Dark hair. Blue eyes. Even sideburns. For a moment she wondered if he expected her to curtsy before him as if he were some kind of feudal lord.

His gaze swept her up and down. "I see you made it in one piece."

He looked for flaws, no doubt, although he would find

none in the tasteful jeans and long-sleeved brown cotton shirt she wore.

"I sure did."

"Pleasant drive?"

"Pleasant enough."

She'd come to California straight from Nevada where her best friend, Trent Anderson, had won the team roping average at the National Finals Rodeo with his longtime roping partner, Mac. That left her exactly two weeks to plan Trent's wedding, something that seemed like an impossible task, especially without his bride, Alana McClintock, around. The two of them had flown home to meet Trent's mother. That meant she was on her own with nobody but Alana's best friend, Cabe, and Cabe's daughter, Rana, to help her out. To top it off, she'd never planned a wedding before in her life, but it couldn't be that hard, right? And she had the food thing dialed-in thanks to the catering business she used to own. All she had to do was make arrangements for a wedding hall. Flowers shouldn't be too hard. Party favors. Centerpieces. Decorations. She could handle all that, and the cake....

"You need some help?" Cabe stared pointedly at her car.

She glanced at the three pieces of luggage in her trunk—two suitcases, a matching toiletry bag and a garment bag that contained the dress she would wear to Trent and Alana's wedding, bought in Las Vegas, of course. Enough clothes for three weeks. "No, no, I've got it."

"Here." He darted down the steps.

The man didn't know how to take no for an answer. She quickly pulled the last piece of luggage out—the small toiletry case—hoping to scoop everything up before he got there, but she should have known better. He was by her side in an instant.

"Let me have that." He grabbed the handle of her largest suitcase before she could stop him.

"You don't need to do that."

She was treated to his censorious stare beneath the brim of his black cowboy hat—one that matched his shirt—but that wasn't curled up around the rim like a traditional hat. In this part of the country, everyone wore them wide and flat. They might look silly on some cowboys, but not Cabe. Too handsome for his own good, she thought, not for the first time.

"Thanks," she said, cursing inside because she'd meant the word to come out sounding truly thankful, but it'd come out all wrong—more grudging than grateful.

"My pleasure."

He didn't like her. She'd known that, although it didn't make it any easier to swallow. She knew why, too. From the moment she'd first spotted Cabe Jensen standing in the middle of a barn aisle five months ago, she'd become a babbling moron. She hadn't meant to sound so domineering and bossy, but she knew that's exactly how her words had come off to his ears. She'd tried to rectify the situation at least a half dozen times, but every time she opened her mouth she said the wrong thing all over again. Drove her nuts.

"And thanks so much for letting me stay with you." She really *was* grateful about that. It would make things much easier.

"It's going to be great." His smile looked as sickly as a cardiac patient's. "I can't wait."

She almost laughed. Acting would never be his forte. "I can't wait, either."

He glanced back at her. She felt her cheeks flush with heat. The man had that effect on her. That, too, drove her nuts.

"I, ah…" She smiled. "It's going to be a lot of work, of course. You know. The whole wedding in two weeks thing, but it'll be easier with your help."

There. That hadn't sounded too bad.

He picked up the last of her luggage and turned to face her. She almost laughed all over again. Poor man looked like a pack mule with her luggage stacked beneath his arms.

"Don't count on me for much help. You're the pro." He headed for the house before she could stop him. "And I hope you can pull it off for Alana and Trent's sake," he added over his shoulder.

Thanks for the vote of confidence, she found herself thinking. Typical Cabe. He was Alana's boss and best friend, and so she bit back a sarcastic retort, but it was hard.

He paused at the top of the steps, glancing back at her. "Coming?"

She'd been staring after him like a buffoon. "I need to get my cat."

"Excuse me?"

Oh, dear. He hadn't been told. Darn that Alana and Trent. They should have given him a heads-up.

"Ramses." She smiled sheepishly. "My cat. After the pharaoh. He thinks he's king of the world, and if I'd left him behind in Colorado, he wouldn't have spoken to me for a month. Seriously. He has major catt-itude. Didn't Alana and Trent tell you I was bringing him along?"

Clearly not.

"I hate cats."

Big surprise. He probably hated puppies, babies and fuzzy little chicks, too. "I promise you won't even notice him."

His lips tightened in a way that projected "Famous last words."

Oh, well. Nothing she could do about it now. It wasn't like she could ship Ramses home.

"You'll see. He's adorable. Nobody can resist Ramses."

Nobody but him, she would bet.

She headed toward the front seat of the rental where Ramses had spent the past few hours riding it out—much to his dismay. The orange Peke-faced Persian stared up at her in the same way Cabe Jensen did—with a combination of resentment and disgust.

"Hey there, buddy." She lifted the travel kennel up to her face. Ramses's gaze moved from her to the pasture behind her, then back to her face again, pupils flaring, smooshed-in nose lifting up as if he'd caught a whiff of the pines and freshly cut grass behind her. "You okay?"

As a reply, the cat let out his trademark Persian howl, a cross between stepped-on kitty and wailing banshee. Her gaze darted to Cabe, but he just raised his brows and shook his head.

"Great," she thought she heard him mutter.

Relax, she told herself. It wasn't as though she and Ramses would be seeing a lot of the man. He was the proprietor of a guest ranch, one that specialized in people with disabilities. This time of year the ranch catered to a different type of clientele, Alana had told her: big-game hunters. According to Alana it was a booming business. Elk and antelope and a whole host of other animals made their home in the high California desert.

"Got anything else in there I need to know about?" he asked.

"Nope." She cradled Ramses's cage in front of her. "This is the last surprise."

This time, she was certain she heard him grunt. "I hope so."

She hoped so, too.

HE COULD FEEL her behind him.

Stubborn, opinionated woman. Why wasn't he surprised she'd brought along her cat? And what the hell was in the suitcases he lugged up the steps of his home? Damn things weighed as much as a ship anchor.

"Wow. This is pretty, Cabe."

Hadn't she been in his home before? He frowned.

Now that he thought about it, she hadn't. He'd given her a wide berth when she'd visited the ranch last summer.

"How long have you lived here?"

"All my life," he said, struggling to get the multiple pieces of luggage up the first flight of stairs. It was like carrying bales of hay, and it took everything he had to keep his breathing under control. Damned if he'd let her see him struggle.

"You sure you don't want help with that?" she asked, almost as if she read his mind.

"Just hold on to your cat."

"Not my hat?"

He glanced back down at her. She smiled up at him. He decided to ignore her.

She wouldn't let him. "The house looks really old."

He paused for a moment, ostensibly so he could respond to her comment, but really so he could catch his breath at the top of the steps. He felt as if his arms had stretched two inches by the time he set her luggage down.

"It was built in 1859," he all but wheezed.

"No kidding."

At the bottom of the steps was the family room, the

hardwood floor so shiny it reflected the image of a massive stone fireplace that sat kitty-corner from the front door. Claw-footed furniture was arranged around the room, a beige-and-brown cowhide lay in the middle of the floor, matching pillows on the sofa. Across from the family room, still along the front of the house, was a drawing room, and behind that, toward the back, the kitchen overlooked a side pasture that stretched all the way to the main road.

"Our family was one of the first to settle in the area."

"Neat."

At the look of approval in her eyes, he picked up the luggage again. Sure, he was normally a lot friendlier to his guests, and sure, he was probably a bit hard on her, but Saedra Robbins annoyed the heck out of him with her I-can-do-anything-you-can-do attitude. That was why he'd be boiled in hoof tar before he let her see how out of breath he was.

One step at a time.

"Where are you taking me?"

"Attic."

He heard her laugh. "Going to lock me in there?"

Now *there* was an idea. Granted, Trent and Alana might not approve, but it sure would make his life easier. She rubbed him the wrong way, but he was also man enough to admit that part of his problem was how *gorgeous* the woman was. Not just mildly pretty. Not even vaguely pretty. She was breathtakingly beautiful with her wide blue eyes, full lips and heart-shaped face that featured a tiny button nose and softly rounded chin.

"Not unless you misbehave." He was only half-kidding.

Maybe things wouldn't have been so bad if he'd had a spare cabin for her to stay in, but with the ranch fully booked, it'd made sense to have her stay in his home. Frankly, it'd been the only option. Even the hotels were booked this time of year.

"Hmm." Her long blond hair fell over one shoulder as she pretended to consider his words. "That sounded like a challenge."

Was she flirting with him? He drew himself up as best he could considering his burden, arranging his face into a mask of indifference. She would learn he had no interest in women, not even a beautiful one. His damn sexual attraction was just an annoyance—nothing more.

"It was meant as a warning."

He'd made it to the top of the steps, thank God, and he breathed a sigh of relief. Funny that she could stand beneath him on the steps, smaller by at least a foot, and yet he could still feel the urge to run away.

"Did you hear that, Ramses?" She turned the cage around so she could peer at her cat. She pitched her voice down low and gruff. "We've been warned."

This would be a long couple of weeks, he thought, turning back to the task at hand. At least she was a full floor away. And with life on the ranch as busy as it was, what with livestock management and guests to entertain, he'd see very little of her.

He hoped.

"Here you go."

He left the luggage outside her room before swinging open a door. The roofline was lower here, but only along the front of the house. It sloped upward, toward the middle of the home, allowing for two dormers, one to the left and one to the right and each with a bench seat and a puffy pillow in front of it. The perfect place to sit and daydream…or write.

He backed away from that thought like a horse spooking at a plastic bag.

"Wow." She brushed past him, the air she disturbed leaving behind the scent of vanilla and cinnamon. Gently, she set her cat down on the daybed to her right. "This is stunning."

Blue. His wife's favorite color. On the walls, billowing down in drapes, echoed in the quilt on the bed.

Why hadn't he been up here before now? Why had he waited until it was time to show Saedra to her room to make the trek upstairs?

So you could put off facing Kimberly's hideaway and be reminded of her and all that you lost.

"Enjoy." He brushed past her.

"Wait!" He heard her take a few steps. "Where's the bathroom?"

"Out the door, to the right."

He couldn't get away fast enough.

"But I thought we could go over a few things. You know, for the wedding."

He should have let her stay in one of the guest bedrooms. He shouldn't have allowed her up here. And he definitely should have ignored his instincts to keep her far away.

"Can't," he shot over his shoulder. *Keep walking.* "Things to do."

"Cabe."

Ignore her. Don't look back. There's no need to pretend you like the woman. She's not a guest.

But years of playing the polite host proved impossible to ignore. He paused near the top step, slowly turned to face her despite the inner warnings to do the exact opposite. The sight of her standing there, sunlight framing her silhouette, blond hair set aglow—it did things to his insides.

So much like Kimberly.

Saedra was taller, of course, but everything else seemed the same, from the length of her hair to the shape of her body, even down to what she wore: the stone-washed jeans and formfitting long-sleeved top. He could just picture Kim standing there, a smile on her face as she chastised him for interrupting her while she'd been in the midst of writing. Usually those interruptions led to something else, something that would quickly change her teasing grin into sighs of pleasure....

"I just want to say thanks again for inviting me to stay in your home." She rubbed her hands together, as if nervous. "I know you and I don't exactly see eye-to-eye, but I promise to make this as painless as possible."

It wasn't her fault he'd never gotten over the death of his wife. Not her fault at all.

Run.

He turned away before he could say something he might regret because although he might not be interested in women, his body didn't seem to know it. And that presented one tiny little problem.

He was attracted to her.

"I'll see you at dinner," she called out after him.

Not if he could help it.

Chapter Two

"This is going to be fun."

Saedra glanced at the fourteen-year-old girl who sat across from her. Cabe's daughter, as different from Cabe in personality as sunlight was from darkness, resembled her father with the same brown hair and blue eyes.

"I sure hope so," Saedra said, eyeing the clock. Two hours until dinnertime. Maybe she'd get lucky and he wouldn't put in an appearance. "But I'm starting to wonder if I bit off more than I can chew."

They were in the kitchen, a spacious room that overlooked the front pasture thanks to an octagon window where a bar-height kitchen table sat. Not for the first time Seadra found herself wondering how Cabe could have such a delightful daughter and be such a stink-butt himself.

"What do you need help with?" Rana jiggled in her chair, her brown braids falling over the front of her shoulders. She didn't wear her cowboy hat, but she'd been wearing one when she'd gotten off the bus at the end of the driveway an hour or so ago. Saedra had watched her walk up the long road from where she and Ramses had settled on one of the pillow cushions next to the window. She'd been writing her to-do list for the wedding, but she liked the young girl. A friendly face. She needed that.

"Everything." Saedra played with the notepad she'd used. Scrawled in her loopy handwriting was a list a mile long, or so it seemed. She sighed. "I guess the first thing to do is decide where we should have it."

"Here."

Saedra tried not to laugh. "Not possible, kiddo. Half the rodeo world will be attending, and you don't have the room. You should have seen everyone at the finals—they can't wait to watch Trent get hitched. Frankly, there's no need to send out invitations because everyone who's anyone is already planning to attend."

The girl tapped her fingers on the side of her cheek, sunlight from the nearby windows making her blue eyes appear huge. "We can rent a tent."

"What if it snows?"

"Then it'll be a white wedding."

Oh, if only it were that simple.

"The weight of the snow will collapse the tent."

"Then we can move the wedding into the horse barn."

"It's not big enough."

"Then I think we're hosed."

Hosed? She almost laughed. She hadn't heard that term in ages. "I think we are, indeed, *hosed.*"

"No, really, Saedra. We're in trouble. There's no place in town where you can have a wedding on such short notice. It'll be Christmas week. The churches will all be having events. So will any of the other usual places. And we don't have a big hotel with a big wedding hall. It's going to have to be here. Plus, I think Alana wants it that way, however we manage to do it."

The kid had a point.

Saedra wrinkled her nose. "Okay, fine. I'll call Alana up and ask her for her thoughts." She made a note in the margin of her list. "What about flowers? Any florists in town?"

"Actually, two."

Woo-hoo. Such a variety.

"I can do the wedding cake myself if I have to, although I prefer not to," Saedra muttered. "But I'm a little stuck on the menu. I would offer to barbecue, but once again, the weather—"

"You need to talk to my dad about cooking. He's really awesome in the kitchen. He had to learn after my mom died."

The sadness that flitted across the girl's face was like a wisp of fog, gone before it could fully form, but still there. Saedra's throat sprouted a lump. Poor thing. She should really cut Cabe some slack. He'd been through a lot.

"Is there a phone book I can use?"

Rana stared at her as if she was speaking a foreign language. "Phone book?"

"Yeah. You know. The yellow book with newspaper pages with numbers on them." She sent the girl a teasing smile.

"No, but there's Google."

"Do you have internet?"

"Of course." Rana gave her a look that clearly said the Jensens weren't complete rednecks. "But I think you should go into town with my dad. You know, see what you can find. Maybe one of the Lions Club halls would work if it's not being used."

Not on her life—at least as far as going anywhere with her dad.

"That's okay." She tried for a sunny smile, although she wasn't entirely certain if she succeeded. "I think I'll wing it on my own. How far is town from here?"

A perplexed frown filled the girl's face. "You passed it on your way here."

That was town? Oh, dear. She'd thought for sure she'd missed a turnoff and that there was a big shopping mall and a residential area somewhere off in the distance. This might be more difficult than she imagined.

"What's the next biggest town?"

"Maybe Susanville." Rana swept a lock of brown hair off her face. "Or Reno."

Reno. That might be an option. She'd driven through there on her way to New Horizons Ranch.

"Okay, great. I'm off, then."

"Not without my dad."

Saedra tucked her chair in, the legs screeching on the hardwood floors. "I don't need your dad."

"What if you get lost?"

"How can I get lost? There's only one road."

"There's other businesses tucked off side streets." The girl jumped off her stool. "Dad!" She turned toward the front of the house. "Saedra needs to go into town."

"No," Saedra cried, holding out her hands. "That's okay. I can explore on my own."

"Da-ad!" Rana called again.

"It's okay, Rana. Really. No need to bother—"

"What's all the yelling about?"

Crud. He must have been right around the corner.

"Saedra needs you to take her into town," the girl announced.

The man filled the doorway, and without his cowboy hat, his brown wavy hair made him appear more boyish. Not at all what she would have expected.

"Actually, I'll be fine on my own."

"But you don't know where anything is." Rana met her

father's gaze. "She needs to visit the florist and maybe stop off at someplace that rents tents."

"No, no." Saedra pulled out her cell phone. "I'll be fine on my own." She shot him a smile. "Have Google, will travel."

Cabe's lips lifted, but not into a smile. No. More of a grimace. She could tell he searched for a graceful way out of his daughter's request, but couldn't think of anything.

"What time did you want to leave?"

She released a sigh of disappointment. "Really, Cabe. It's okay. I'm sure you have a million things to do, what with guests arriving tomorrow—"

"Don't listen to her, Dad. She's trying to be polite, but we don't have time for that. Trent and Alana's wedding is in two weeks."

And somewhere in there was Christmas, as Rana had mentioned. Come to think of it, where were all the Christmas decorations? Not so much as a jingle bell in sight.

"I can take you to town in an hour."

"Perfect!" Rana couldn't contain her excitement. "I'll stay here and research outdoor weddings. Maybe someone can rent us a portable building or something."

Saedra spun to face the little girl. "You're not going with us?" She was certain her panic showed on her face.

"Nah. I have some homework to do. But I stay here alone all the time. No need to look so worried."

Worried was not the word. *Dismayed.* Maybe even *nauseous.*

"In fact, I think I'll get started on that homework now." Rana reached for a bowl of apples sitting on a rose-colored countertop. "I'll see you after."

Only if Saedra didn't run screaming for the hills.

NOT EVEN AN hour had passed and already she'd interfered with his life.

Relax, Cabe, it's not like she doesn't have a good reason.

Cabe tried to remind himself of that fact as he pulled up in front of his home. His daughter had had a point earlier. The sooner they got the major details of Alana's wedding done, the sooner Saedra would be out of his hair. He was certain the woman could manage the minor details on her own.

He hoped.

She came bounding down the steps of his house like a teenager and looking younger than her years in her off-white jacket and a matching knit hat that hugged the contours of her face. The sun had already started to set, golden rays of light catching the twin edges of her pigtails and setting them afire. Pigtails. It should look stupid on someone her age, but on Saedra Robbins, it only made her look sexy. Just the sight of her sent a jolt through his insides, one that left him feeling flushed and edgy and out of sorts.

She jerked on the door handle, the loss in cabin pressure popping his ears, the smell of her assaulting his senses an instant later. Vanilla and cinnamon.

She didn't even bother to greet him. "You don't have to do this."

It must have been his own internal grumpiness that made him say, "I wouldn't if I didn't want to."

She'd slipped into the interior of the ranch's black truck easily, the cabin pressure lowering once again as she slammed the door closed, that space between them suddenly smelling entirely too good for his peace of mind.

"You're just saying that to be kind."

Yes, he was, but she didn't need to know that.

"Rana will understand if we tell her you changed your mind."

"Actually, I think my daughter will make my life miserable if I don't do exactly as she asks."

She frowned. He faced ahead, squinting his eyes against the sunlight on the truck's hood.

"Okay, fine."

He put the truck in gear, trying not to spin the tires as they set off down the drive.

"What's on your list of things to do?"

He could sense her staring at him. He refused to look at her because if he did, he might start thinking those crazy thoughts again, the ones that made his body do things it shouldn't be doing.

You're hard up, buddy.

Maybe he was. That had to be the reason he clenched the steering wheel so hard. Why he refused to look at her. Why he tried not to even breathe deeply. It sure as hell had nothing to do with wanting to go to bed with the woman. She'd be the last woman on earth he'd want to do that with, for myriad reasons. They were polar opposites in personality. He liked things nice and quiet, had worked hard to carve out a routine life that revolved around his ranch and catering to guests. She was used to living life in the limelight. And next year she was making a bid for the National Finals Rodeo on her barrel-racing horse....

Nope. Never in a million years would he be interested in a woman like Saedra Robbins.

"Speaking of the wedding, why don't you have any Christmas decorations up?"

He almost slammed on the brakes. They were at the end of his driveway.

"Did you not have the time because of the NFR?"

He gripped the steering wheel even harder, probably leaving dents, his knuckles screaming in protest.

"Hey. You okay?"

"Fine." He had to force the word past his lips.

"You look sort of...ill."

Deep breath. "We don't decorate the house."

Cabe turned left, out of his driveway, but he could still feel her staring at him, still tell by the way she shifted in her seat that the words surprised her.

"Why not?"

He scanned the road left and right, the waning sunlight causing him to have to lower the brim of his hat so he could see better. "We just don't."

But he knew the moment he said the words that they'd only leave her more curious. He wasn't exactly holding true to his vow to appear more friendly, now, was he?

"Is it a religious thing?"

"No."

"Okay, good, because if it's just a timing thing, I can help. Now would be a really good time to do it, too, you know, before things get too crazy with the wedding."

"No."

"No to doing it now? Or no to decorating entirely?"

"I don't want the house decorated."

Silence. He could sense her surprise. Off in the distance he noticed storm clouds, and Cabe mentally cursed under his breath. In all the hullabaloo surrounding her arrival he hadn't bothered to check the weather forecast. If it was going to snow, that meant he needed to prepare, but by the time he returned from town, it'd be pitch-black outside.

She still hadn't spoken and he knew he'd probably been too harsh. But, damn it, she needed to get it through her head that Christmas was not a good time of year. Not since…

He swallowed.

Kimberly.

"Your wife and brother died around this time of year, didn't they?"

It felt like he'd been sucker punched. As if she'd probed an old wound that sent spasms of pain through his insides. Physical pain.

"I don't want to talk about it."

He stared straight ahead still, but he spotted movement, nearly gasped when he felt her hand on his thigh a moment later.

"Cabe, I'm so, so sorry. I didn't mean… I wasn't trying to…"

What? Be nosy? No. She wasn't trying to be that. He knew that, but he still wanted to lash out at her, had to take deep breaths to keep from saying something he knew he might regret later.

"If it helps, I know what you're going through."

Oh, yeah? Had she lost a wife and a brother on the same day? Had she lost the mother of her only child? Her best friend?

"Dustin died just before the NFR and so, for me, Thanksgiving is hell."

Dustin. Trent's best friend. And hers, too, from the sound of it.

"I didn't mean to pry."

She released his thigh. He closed his eyes against the pain, but it wasn't just emotional pain. Something else had filled him, something that had to do with the way her hand felt against his leg, something that made him so instantly upset, he found himself gunning the engine.

"Let's just get this over with, shall we?"

He headed toward town, glancing back at her in time to see her nod.

But deep down inside, in a place Cabe had forgotten existed, a place that reminded him that he was a man who'd been without a woman for far too long, Cabe wanted to cry. Admitting that he was human, that he found Saedra attractive, was the worst thing of all.

He betrayed his wife with every damn thought.

Chapter Three

They couldn't get to town soon enough.

The man could reduce her comfort level to that of sitting on lava rocks.

Let's just get this over with, shall we?

Maybe she should give him tit for tat. Maybe she should spoon him a taste of his own medicine. Maybe she should make *him* feel as uncomfortable as he made her feel.

When they pulled to a stop in front of a cute little place that had obviously been converted from a single-story house into a florist shop, she smiled brightly and asked, "You're coming in with me, right?"

His eyes widened, his face rearranging itself into that of a man who'd just been told he would receive a tetanus shot. "I wasn't planning on it."

He wore his black cowboy hat again, and to be honest, it really did make his eyes look ridiculously pretty. They were so light. So startling in color. It wasn't fair that eyes such as his should be wasted on such a sourpuss of a man.

"You should come. You're Alana's best friend. You know her better than I do."

Nope. Not a happy camper. Good.

"Fine."

Fine, she mimicked in her own head, happy to escape the truck.

The low-slung home had been painted purple, sparkly Christmas lights surrounding the perimeter of a large picture window in front. Inside she could see refrigerators full of flowers and large plants everywhere. When she opened the door, her nose picked up the scent of eucalyptus and roses. It made her smile for some silly reason.

"I just love roses," she said, looking into his handsome face and seeing his frown. "Do you think Alana likes them, too?"

"No."

Terrific. Maybe this hadn't been such a bright idea, after all.

"Ooo-kay... So what kind of flowers does she like?"

She saw him peek around the shop, saw his gaze settle on some giant Christmas baskets wrapped in cellophane, then move on to a basket of flowers with giant red mums and light green fern.

"There." He pointed. "Sort of like those."

Okay. It was a start.

"Can I help you?" asked a perky-looking blonde with ultrashort hair that featured a streak of red nearly the same shade as the flowers.

"Actually, yes." Saedra approached the front counter. "I need to order flowers for a wedding."

The woman smiled brightly. "Okay, great. We have a book right here of arrangements if you want to look it over." She pulled what appeared to be a photo album from behind the counter. "When is the wedding?"

The moment of truth. "Um. In a couple weeks."

Lips painted ruby-red dropped open revealing a pierced tongue that caught Saedra's attention. Then she said, "You're kidding, right?"

Saedra winced. "Um, no."

"How many arrangements were you thinking?"

"How many can you squeeze in?" Cabe asked for her.

"How big is the bridal party?" the clerk asked.

"Not big." Saedra smiled encouragingly. "We need a bouquet for the bride and something for the maid of honor and a groomsman, and maybe some flowers for centerpieces and whatnot."

The words seemed to kill the deal because the woman shook her head. "Under normal circumstances it wouldn't be an issue, but we've been slammed. One of the biggest businesses in town is having a huge Christmas party for their employees, and we have our regular orders, plus a few other parties. Sorry. But I really don't think we can do it."

Saedra told herself not to panic. There was still the one other florist in town, and if that failed, the local grocery store.

"All right, thanks."

On her way to the door, she stopped at a display of Christmas ornaments, tiny angels dangling from bright red strings, glass balls covered with glitter, twinkling lights glinting off it all.

"Aren't those pretty?"

Cabe had already left the shop. She felt her own mouth drop open, watched as he climbed into his black truck, before glancing back at the tree. How sad that Christmas no longer held any joy for him. No wonder he was always in a grumpy mood.

"You might try Reynolds Florist shop on Second Street," the clerk said.

"Thanks. I'll do that."

A half hour later, she knew it was useless. "Maybe I

could pick some wildflowers," she muttered. "I'm sure there's some up in the hills, right?"

"You'll have to get them from Reno or Susanville."

"Why? Wildflowers don't grow locally?" she teased.

He blinked, glanced down at her, then frowned. "I meant the flowers."

"You don't like my wildflowers idea?"

"There's no wildflowers up in the hills this time of year."

No sense of humor, either. What a mess. At least she had some experience with his type of problem. Her best friend, Trent, had been in a similar frame of mind after the accident that had claimed the life of their mutual best friend, Dustin, and nearly taken Trent's own life, too. Trent had only learned to walk again with Alana's help, which was how they'd all met, only Trent seemed light-years ahead of Cabe emotionally.

"So maybe we can make a bridal bouquet out of papier-mâché?"

Blank stare.

"Or Christmas bows." She sat up straighter. "Speaking of that, I wonder if Alana wants a bachelorette party? You know of any good strip clubs?"

She was just joking, of course, hoping to get a rise out of him. He just started the truck and asked, "Where to next?"

"Hell in a handbasket?"

He glared.

"I guess the local rental place." She kept from rolling her eyes, but only just barely. "There is a rental place around here, isn't there?"

"There is." He put the truck in gear. "Doubt they rent tents."

Cabe the Cheerless. Her new nickname for him.

"Maybe they rent holiday cheer."

He about gave himself whiplash. "Excuse me?"

"Kidding, kidding." She lifted a hand. "Drive on, Jeeves."

FANCIED HERSELF A COMEDIAN, did she? Too bad he didn't feel much like laughing—at least not while she was around.

"Is there a place that sells meat by the bulk, too? I was thinking I could cook a tri-tip dinner."

The sun had sunk below the horizon, reminding Cabe of the time. Would the rental place even be open? Just after five and already the sun was down. He hated this time of year.

"There's a local butcher's shop. He might have some ideas."

"Good. We could go there, too."

He nearly closed his eyes. He had no idea what the hell was wrong with him, but every time she was near he had the darnedest time concentrating on anything but her shapely curves. It was as if he'd been injected with teenage hormones, and frankly, he didn't like it. Not one bit.

"Anyplace else you'd like to see?"

"Weeell, the Eiffel Tower and maybe Westminster Abbey, but I figure I'll get to Europe someday. No need to go now."

She was jerking his chain again, of course, and he wished he knew why the heck her sense of humor always drove him nuts, too. Between his inability to keep his mind off how good she smelled, and her caustic quips, he would have liked to turn the truck around and go home.

"What about a craft store?" She stared at some sort of list she'd written up. "Do you have one of those? Might as well get it over with."

"If you're thinking fake flowers for Alana's wedding, she wouldn't like that."

"Ah!" she said so loudly that it nearly startled him. "An actual opinion. Thank you!"

Smart-ass.

The words were on the edge of his lips, ready to tumble into the abyss of rude comments. Instead, he gripped the wheel and headed for the rental company.

They didn't rent tents.

The owner—a baldheaded man who seemed only too happy to ogle Saedra indefinitely—suggested a party rental place Cabe had never heard of. Alas, that meant another trip across town, only to be told *they* didn't rent tents, either. They suggested a local men's club that had their own tents, which they sometimes rented. So that prompted yet *another* trip across town, but that turned out to be a dead end, too.

"I give up," Saedra said, flopping into the passenger seat of his truck a half hour later.

"Thank God."

She glared. He glared back. She smiled. He looked away.

"I guess it's plastic flowers and rain ponchos for everyone." She was joking, of course, he could see that, and it was damn hard to keep his lips from smiling in return. "Maybe we could hand out umbrellas for wedding favors."

"Please, no."

The smile grew, and from nowhere came the thought that she reminded him of the young fillies he used to break for a local rancher. Obstinate and pigheaded at times, but a heart of gold deep inside. She really was taking her duties seriously, and she was clearly crushed that it wasn't all coming together.

"Seriously, I need to go to a craft store to look for wedding favors."

"We could always get jelly beans and bubblegum balls." He didn't know where the words came from, but he was glad to hear her chuckle.

"You're okay with gum balls but not plastic flowers. Who knew?"

His lips smiled, but they did so without his permission. He forced them back into a pinched line.

"Next you'll suggest frozen pizza and hot dogs for dinner," she added.

He didn't *want* to like her.

He'd spent the past hour trying to ignore how appealing she was only to realize it was more than her physical good looks. It was the sparkle in her eyes, too.

Kimberly had had the same sparkle.

"Speaking of dinner." He saw her take a deep breath, watched as she turned in her seat and faced him, giving him a smile. "How about we grab a bite to eat?"

Chapter Four

"No."

Saedra tried not to let his single-word retort get her down. So what if he didn't want to go to dinner? No reason to cry over it. Not that she was crying, mind you; it just surprised her that right when she thought she'd made some progress, he'd gone back to his old self.

Face it. You're not used to rejection.

It sounded completely egotistical, but it was, in truth, a fact of life that she attracted male attention...lots of male attention. This had cost her many female friendships over the years, so much so that she'd taken to having male friends, like Trent and Mac, rather than deal with all the drama. And now here was a man who clearly didn't like her.

"No problem. Let's head to the craft store," she said.

He didn't go into the store with her. Didn't so much as look at her when she climbed back into the car empty-handed.

"No gum balls," she said.

He started the truck's engine. She gave up. Clearly, she fought a losing battle.

They arrived back at the ranch shortly thereafter, Saedra armed with a list of things to ask Alana, but she was sidetracked by Rana the moment she entered through the door.

"Ohmygosh." The teenager tugged her toward a room toward the back of the house, Cabe all but sprinting past her and disappearing to goodness knew where. "I found the perfect tent for Alana's wedding."

She opened the door to a room that was clearly Cabe's study, a room filled with books, something that brought Saedra up short. Gorgeous brown oak shelves matched a desk in front of a giant picture window, and Saedra caught a glimpse of their reflections in the glass thanks to the darkness outside.

"I've been looking online and it turns out there's a place that rents tents in Reno, which is only a couple of hours away, but the website says they deliver, and so I called, but they were closed already, but if you look right here…"

Rana still had ahold of her arms, twin braids nearly slapping Saedra in the face as the girl spun to face the computer, her fingers tapping the keyboard of a sleek laptop.

"See?"

After the dismal few hours she'd just spent, it was a balm to Saedra's soul to witness the girl's enthusiasm. Maybe her stay at the Jensen household wouldn't be so bad, after all.

"Don't you love it?"

She would have to admit, the tent looked perfect for their purposes, though it didn't look a thing like a traditional tent, more like the Swiss Alps with its multiple peaks and steep edges.

"It says the tent's designed to repel snow off the edges and that they have portable heaters you can rent, too."

Saedra hadn't known how tense she was until she expelled a deep sigh of relief. "It's perfect."

A squeal leaked out of the girl just before she turned and gave her a hug.

"Do we know how much?" Saedra asked, leaning toward the screen.

"No price."

That didn't bode well.

"But Trent said cost wasn't an issue, remember?"

Yeah, but there was cost and then there was *cost*.

"Let's see what else they have."

They cruised around the website, Saedra spying several tents that might work. They also rented tables and chairs and chafing dishes, silverware and plates—everything they needed.

"One-stop shopping." Saedra turned to Rana. "Good job, kiddo. This place looks perfect. I'll call them tomorrow."

"My mom used them once." The little girl lost her smile for a moment. "We had a fundraiser out here for my school before…"

Her world had been turned upside down. Alana had told her about it. Cabe's wife and brother had been killed and Rana critically injured. Rana had lost the use of her legs. They'd thought she'd never walk again, but Alana had taken on the role of therapist. They'd used horses to strengthen Rana's legs. It was how New Horizons Ranch had gotten its start. Alana had found her calling and Cabe had found something to keep his mind off his loss, or so Saedra surmised.

"It must have been hard," Saedra found herself saying, "what you went through."

It broke her heart to see the pain on Rana's face. "Harder for my dad." Saedra saw the girl take a deep breath before meeting her gaze. "I was out of it for the first few months. They had me on a lot of medication. But my dad…" She shook her head. "He had to take care of…everything."

She'd missed her mom's funeral. Alana had told her that, too. Poor Rana had been bed bound for months. Cabe had made all the arrangements. He'd had Alana for support, the two of them grieving together, but it'd been a horrible time, Alana had admitted. No wonder Cabe was such a curmudgeon.

"And now here we are." She touched the girl's arm lightly. "Planning a wedding."

The smile returned, although not as brightly. "It's going to be fun."

Fun.

That's what the Jensens needed, Alana thought. Fun. They were both stuck in the past. Oh, sure, they appeared to have moved on, what with starting New Horizons Ranch and opening their home to strangers, but their pain was still there, bubbling beneath the surface. It tugged at Alana's heartstrings and she vowed to do whatever she could to help them both.

"You know what I think?"

Rana's gaze hooked her own. "What?"

"I think we need to decorate the house for Christmas."

"Oh, no. We couldn't do that. My dad, he wouldn't—"

"Approve," Alana finished for her. "I know." Just as she knew she had to tread carefully, too. "But how would *you* feel if the house was decorated?"

Rana's smile brightened again. "I would love it." She seemed almost ashamed to admit it, though. "I miss Christmas."

She was still a child for all her outward appearance. A

teenager, yes, but still young enough to be excited about presents and stockings and Christmas cheer.

"We should do it," Saedra said.

"My dad—"

"Leave him to me."

Fun.

They needed it *bad,* and she was just the person to show them how it was done.

HE MANAGED TO avoid Saedra the next day, which wasn't hard to accomplish with guests in residence. All it took was the offer of a guided hunt and one of his best customers, a dealership owner from the city, leaped at the chance. Cabe leaped at the opportunity to leave the ranch.

He was gone all day. When he returned later that afternoon, it was to note every light in his house ablaze and the sound of music thumping through the window.

"Damn."

He thought about turning around. There was always work to do in the barn. He could sweep out the feed room or rearrange the saddles, maybe muck some stalls.

His empty belly put a stop to such thoughts. It was his house and he'd be damned if he allowed a woman to scare him out of it.

The music coming from his study nearly deafened him, Cabe counseling himself to take it easy on Rana. Sometimes he forgot that she was a teenager and that blaring music at unhealthy levels was a rite of passage.

But it wasn't Rana who was playing the music.

He drew up short in the doorway as Saedra glanced up, a smile unfurling across her face like the petals on a flower. She was seated behind his desk, a fuzzy off-white sweater with a cowl neckline hugging a body that belonged in a Victoria's Secret catalog. Her long blond hair hung loose around her shoulders as she swung the chair from side to side. She half closed the screen of the laptop Rana must have allowed her to borrow.

"There you are," she said, but she had to yell to be heard. "I was wondering when you'd get back."

"Here I am," he repeated back faintly. The truth was, the sight of her sitting there had completely poleaxed him.

"How was the great safari?"

He was so befuddled he heard himself ask, "Safari?"

"Your big-game hunt." She fashioned a pistol out of her fingers, mimicked the sound of a gun. "Bag any big ones?" The pistol morphed into an antler at the side of her head, her other hand joining the first, fingers splayed. "Eight pointers."

He glanced at the stereo, though if he were honest with himself he did so to prevent her from seeing a smile, although why he wanted to keep his grin to himself he had no idea. "Can we turn that down?"

"That," she said over the pounding beat, "is our homework assignment for the night."

Why did he have a feeling he wouldn't like what she had to say?

"We need to choose music for the wedding."

"Can't Alana and Trent choose their own music?"

She tossed him a single shake of her head. "I suppose they could, but I would bet that between the two of us we can do a pretty good job. You know Alana like the back of your hand and I know Trent. Ergo, we can do it ourselves."

When he straightened away from the stereo, the music blissfully silenced, he caught sight of something else. Stacked on a table near one of the bookcases were pink boxes, the kind one found in bakeries and doughnut shops.

"That's our other task." She pointed, giving him an impish smile. "You're going to help me choose a wedding cake."

"No."

"Excuse me?"

He shook his head in case she had really missed his meaning. "I haven't eaten today. The last thing I need is sugar." And loud music, but he kept the last to himself.

"I thought of that." She got up from her seat. "Before Rana left for her friend's house, I made dinner. Fried chicken. One of my other specialties. Go ahead and eat."

"Rana went to a friend's?"

She nodded.

He suddenly felt as though he lost ten pints of blood. "We're alone?"

She made scary fingers. "Yes," she said in what sounded like a Russian accent. "But I promise not to drink your blood."

He blinked, *blood* having come out sounding like *blah-ud*. He almost smiled again.

"When will she be back?"

"She was hoping to spend the night. Said she'd call you later on."

No. That wasn't going to happen. He wasn't spending a night under the same roof as Saedra Robbins. Alone. Just the thought did something to his body that he'd rather not think about.

"Actually, I have to go out tonight."

"No, you don't."

He about did a double take.

"I had Rana check your schedule. You don't have anything planned."

"Rana's not my social director."

"No, but she said you always check in with her. Always."

Busted. "Something came up."

"What?"

None of your business. That's what he wanted to shout. "I need to do some paperwork in my office." He quickly pointed toward the front door. "The one in the barn."

Her face lit up. It was amazing what happened to her eyes when that happened. They practically sparkled. "Okay, good. I can finish downloading the music while you finish up your work."

If he protested any more, he'd end up sounding like a jerk. "Fine."

And that *didn't sound jerklike?*

He silenced himself by leaving. He wasn't really lying. Not really. He always had paperwork to do, but she insisted on sending him off with a plate full of chicken. Once his belly was full, it was hard to resist the urge to hide in his office for the rest of the night, but a beep on his phone, followed by a voice announcing, "I'm done," preempted the notion. Someone had taught her to use the intercom system. Great.

He took his time walking down the steps that ran alongside the back wall of the feed room. The smell of sweetened oats filled his nose, and the quiet nickering of horses soothed his frayed nerves. The twelve-stall barn was only a couple of years old, built when they opened the ranch to visitors, and it housed the horses they used for their therapy program. Fluorescent lights hung from the middle of the barn aisle. Horse heads popped up one by one as he walked by. They'd installed an arena off the front, and to his left and out back behind the barn stretched acres and acres of pasture, but for now he headed right and toward the pathway that led to his house. Through the tall pines he could make out his study light, and above that, Rana's bedroom light. She must have left it on. Darn kid. One of these days he was going to make her pay the power bill.

That sweater of Saedra's really did hug her every curve. He had occasion to notice the moment he walked in the door, since the woman all but bounded out of the kitchen and into the foyer. What the sweater didn't cover, skintight black leggings did, the ends tucked into lamb's fleece and brown suede boots.

"I hope you like sweets."

Only if she was on the menu.

He winced. She didn't seem to notice—she was too busy motioning toward the kitchen and the pink boxes, which she'd moved onto the bar-height kitchen table. "I thought we could listen to the music I downloaded earlier while you do some tasting."

"Terrific."

He couldn't have sounded more sarcastic if he tried. He knew that. Told himself to lighten up a bit. He'd morphed into some kind of computer program that went into nasty default mode whenever she stood near.

"Okay, here we go." His tone of voice didn't appear to get her down. If anything, she seemed to perk up even more, even waved her iPod at him. "Let me just plug this into the player I brought down earlier." She spun toward a long counter that separated the kitchen from his family room. Two seconds later the soft voice of Clint Black filled the room. She turned back to him with a smile. "You like that?"

"I think it's more important that Trent and Alana like it."

"I know, but Trent loves this song, and I just wondered if Alana might like it, too."

"If it's country, she'll like it."

"Perfect." She patted the back of a bar stool. "Now sit."

He cocked his head. "Just cut me a slice and I'll taste."

"Nope." She opened one of the pink boxes. "We're going to have some fun while you do this."

"Fun?"

When she faced him again, long blond hair shimmering, she seemed on the verge of a laugh. "Yes. You remember what fun is, don't you?"

"Of course." What kind of person did she think he was? "I just don't see what it has to do with tasting cake."

"It turns out there's a plethora of bakers in the area. Most of them were kind enough to whip something up for me today given the short notice, so I need you to tell me which of the six cakes you like."

"Six?"

"Yeah, I know. I've already made my choice. Now it's your turn."

He scouted the table. "Where's a fork?"

"Oh, no. I don't want you to see who's made what in case you know these people. I want only the best for Alana and Trent."

"What? You think I'd choose a cake because it's someone I know?"

"You might play favorites, and so I'm going to blindfold you."

He gaped, but only for a moment. "You're out of your mind."

"Come on."

She couldn't be serious.

He glanced at the cake in question. "Just pull them out of the boxes so I can't tell which one came from which store."

She seemed startled by his suggestion. She, too,

glanced at the boxes before turning back to him with a frown. "What's the fun in that?" And she sounded so disappointed it was almost comical. "C'mon." She tipped her head sideways and gave him a look meant to charm him into cooperating. "You need to loosen up. Even Rana thought it was a good idea."

"Then I suggest you play pin the tail on the cake batter with Rana."

She plopped down in the chair next to him, and if he were honest with himself, he could admit to feeling just a little bad about spoiling her mood. Just a little.

"Okay, fine. Open your mouth."

"Excuse me?"

She picked up a fork, opened one of the boxes, then stabbed a piece of cake. "Open."

"I'm not three years old."

"Of course not, but you're still going to do a blind taste test. Well, sort of blind. Here. Open."

She adopted such a look of ferocious determination that he found himself opening his mouth despite himself. Sugar and lemon and vanilla filled his mouth. Cabe suddenly felt self-conscious as he chewed.

"Tastes like cake."

"Ha-ha. Very funny." Her left brow lifted. "Well?"

"I guess it's okay."

She wrinkled her nose. "Wow. What a ringing endorsement. Okay. Next."

Before she could stuff another forkful in his mouth, he lifted a hand. "Why don't you and Rana just decide?"

"Because you're a part of this wedding, too, and with Trent and Alana not here, we're it. So, open."

Once again, he did as instructed even though a voice inside his head told him to put his foot down. Utter nonsense.

But the piece of cake she fed him was *good.*

"Oooh. You like that one, don't you?"

"Wait," he said through a mouth full of white cake with some kind of strawberry frosting that was so good he wanted another bite. "What makes you think I like it?"

She reached for another box. "You're like a newspaper. I can read the headlines from a mile away. Here's another one."

How the hell did she do it? How had she gotten him to eat—almost literally—out of her hand, and why was he fighting so hard to keep his face free of expression as he tasted the next piece?

"You don't like that one, either. Okay. Next."

"What?" He swallowed. Actually, he almost gagged. Ugh. Nasty, greasy frosting. "You didn't even give me time to taste it."

"I could tell the minute your mouth closed, and I don't blame you for disliking that one. I didn't like it, either."

"Ah," he muttered. "So *you're* the one that's biased. See. You should just decide for me."

"I'm not biased. Some of the cakes I really liked and other ones I didn't. Rana, too. You're the tiebreaker."

She held up the fork again. He eyed the piece she was about to feed him. After that last one, he should be more cautious.

"I'm not a big fan of cream fillings," he admitted, eyeing the white cake and white frosting.

"Me, neither, but taste it just the same. You might be surprised."

But she missed, her other hand instantly lifting to help push the cake into his mouth, her fingers grazing his lips.

He nearly gasped.

Zapped by an electric fence, that was what it felt like.

As if a million joules of energy stole his breath away. He froze.

"Well?"

His taste buds failed to function, too. So did his heart. And his lungs.

"Good," he managed to mumble.

"Just good?"

It took every ounce of control not to jerk away. Not to jump to his feet and dash away.

"I like the strawberry one better."

She nodded. He sat there.

What the hell was *that*?

But he knew. *That* was more than mere sexual attraction. *That* was want. *That* was need. *That* was trouble.

Chapter Five

He bolted.

That was the only way to describe what happened after he tasted the last piece of cake. The man didn't even have the common decency to listen to the music she'd downloaded, just offered a flip, "Have Rana do it."

She'd touched him. And it had freaked him out.

She hadn't been kidding when she'd told him she could read his face, so as she climbed into bed that night, she brought up the memory of his face and reexamined every angle.

Instant awareness. Physical attraction. Desire.

It'd been all there, plain as day, and it had taken her completely by surprise as the reason for his animosity became patently clear.

He liked her. *Liked* liked her. As in he wanted her in his bed.

The thought made her giggle like a schoolgirl, and she rolled onto her side, causing Ramses to let out a mew of protest.

"Oh, stop it," she warned the cat. "You know you want to cuddle with me."

The cat started purring, but only after Saedra stroked his back. Silly cat. Typical male. Complain, complain, when really, deep inside, they wanted attention. That was

Cabe's problem, too. She wondered if he was in his own bed, below her, thinking about her.

Of course he was.

That made her giggle some more. It wasn't funny, though, she sternly told herself. The man had issues. Major, major issues that would make him horrible boyfriend material.

She should ignore him.

That's what she told herself as she continued to pet Ramses. Now that she knew he suffered from severe sexual frustration, maybe she should cut him some slack, too. It'd been months since she'd had a sexual partner herself. Actually, more like a year. Who had time for relationships when you ran a successful business like her Buckaroo Barbecue, or his New Horizons Ranch? It was only recently that she'd had time to even think about the opposite sex, and then only in terms of what Trent might like for a wedding present. If she were honest with herself, she could do with some good, old-fashioned sex herself, but not with Cabe.

Why *not* with Cabe?

Stupid, ridiculous thought, she told herself, her eyes drifting closed. Her subconscious picked up on her thoughts about Cabe and ran with it. She dreamed that night: her fantasies featured a dark-haired man with sideburns and a toned upper body that, in her dreams at least, felt as soft as silk yet was as hard as iron.

"This is not good," she told Ramses as she dressed the next morning. The cat sat on the windowsill, cleaning himself in a patch of sunlight, and completely ignoring her. "Not that *you* care."

Rana must have still been asleep, since Saedra encountered only silence as she made her way downstairs. The girl was on Christmas vacation until after the wedding. At least the teenager could serve as a buffer. This morning Saedra needed to call the rental place in Reno. And then there was the issue of Christmas and the decorations, which Rana had told her were stored in the attic. As luck would have it, the entrance was right by her room, through what looked like a pantry door next to the stairwell. Might as well see what they had. The wedding would be on Christmas Day and she planned to do it up right. It wouldn't be a winter wedding without them.

Saedra marveled when she opened the trapdoor. It wasn't really an attic space, but more like a room. Skylights illuminated a crawl space big enough for someone to stand in and wide enough to fit a bed and a dresser. To her left were blue plastic tubs labeled Christmas, Fall, Spring, Summer... Saedra having no doubt they were decorations. To her right were bags of what looked like clothes.

Creeping forward, she peered inside one of them, taking a step back when she realized what they were.

His wife's clothes. Bags and bags of them.

Her stomach curdled with sadness as she looked around, imagining the pain Cabe and Rana must have gone through as they'd bagged up not just Kimberly's things, but Brayden's things, as well. Sure, she'd lost Dustin last year, but he'd been a friend, nothing like losing a wife and a brother on the same day.

"No wonder you're such a mess," she told a Cabe that was nowhere in sight.

Amazing that Rana hadn't been more affected. Alana had told her the girl suffered from horrible nightmares. It was one of the reasons Alana had insisted she and Trent would spend their summers at New Horizons Ranch. Cabe had coped as well as could be expected, Alana had also told her, but clearly his scars ran deep, too. It'd been years since his wife's death. Years. Clearly, he still wasn't over it.

Maybe she could change all that. Maybe what this place needed was her, someone who had lost her parents at a young age, but who had gone on to survive despite her grief. Yes, she'd ended up with a twisted sense of humor. Maybe even a macabre sense of humor, but she'd learned the hard way that death was a part of life. It sucked, but if you didn't move on, it would bring you down.

Like Cabe.

So. Taking a deep breath, she turned toward the boxes. In for a penny, in for a pound. Rana had given her the go-ahead. That was good enough for Saedra. Cabe might not like it, but he'd learn to deal.

An hour later she stood in the middle of Cabe's study, scanning the open tubs of Christmas decorations and wondering where to start.

"What in the hell do you think you're doing?"

She jumped.

"Get the hell away from that stuff."

She'd known this wouldn't be easy, but she actually felt the blood drain from her face at Cabe's tone of voice.

"Hey, Cabe."

Smile.

Beneath his black cowboy hat his blue eyes blazed. He wore a brown Carhartt jacket and matching pants tucked into leather hunting boots, and Saedra thought he couldn't look more masculine—and more furious—if he tried.

Smile bigger.

But it was hard not to blanch. Even beneath his jacket she could tell his shoulders were as tightly stretched as a bow.

Dear me.

"Put. Those. Back."

She glanced down at the boxes. "The Christmas decorations? Why?"

Pretending innocence was not the correct thing to do. That became apparent the moment the words slid from her mouth because, if he'd looked furious before, he appeared positively enraged now.

"You know damn well why."

Yes, she did.

"But we need these to decorate for the wedding."

"No, you don't." His jaw ticked all the way up to his sideburns.

The smile on her face slowly wilted. "But if we don't use Christmas decorations, people might think it strange."

"Get them out of here."

He spun on his heel. Saedra's spine chose that moment to collapse. A few seconds later, she heard his footsteps on the stairway. Boom. Boom. Boom.

"Oh, dear."

That hadn't gone well at all. Actually, she'd been expecting to have the place done by the time he came home. Just her luck that he would pop in before she could even start.

A few moments later she heard his footsteps again and then the slamming of the front door.

"What'd he say?"

She jumped—again.

"All I heard was the booming of his feet," Rana said.

"I think China heard the booming of his feet."

"What'd he say?"

"To put the decorations back."

She noticed the girl's John Deere pajamas, the green-colored fabric sporting yellow tractor logos. She looked so much like her dad it was uncanny, but she had a different nose, likely taking after her mother in that respect. It was a tiny little stub of a thing that made her look younger than her years, especially with her hair pulled back into a ponytail.

"You going to do it?"

"Should I?"

Rana's gaze caught on the boxes, her eyes going dull. "I didn't mean to get you in trouble."

Saedra put her arms around the girl. "It isn't your fault, hon. Not at all. Your dad needs to get over his big, bad self."

"He can be such a grump at times," the teenager muttered.

The words so closely echoed Saedra's own thoughts that she smiled. "It's okay. I can put them back."

"No. Don't."

Saedra drew back, surprised to see the determination in the teenager's face. She looked mature beyond her years all of sudden.

"He's wrong." She motioned to the boxes. "Hiding mom's decorations… It's gone on long enough." She lifted her chin. "My mom would never have wanted us to ignore Christmas."

HE COULDN'T BELIEVE the woman's audacity.

Cabe mashed the pedal of his four-wheel drive vehicle, gravel kicking up by the tires of the trucklike ATV, the winter wind prickling his skin.

Who did she think she was?

His wheels kicked right. He took his foot off the gas, refusing to kill himself because Saedra had crossed the line. The tall pines around him cast triangular patterns on the ground, the air beneath the canopy of needles chilling him to the bone. From the seat next to him he retrieved a pair of leather gloves, taking care to pull them on while navigating the half-mile-long road that led to the cabins. The drive should have soothed him. Usually, the sweeping meadows and the groves of trees reminded him of what he had to be grateful for. Sure, he might have lost his brother and his wife, but he still had Rana—that was a miracle all on its own.

Christmas decorations. After he specifically told her he didn't decorate.

The pathway swept to the right, the road sweeping down a small hill. The vista ahead should have calmed him down, too, with the Pit River to his right, eight cabins on his left, one right next to another, and beyond all that, more meadows and pasture and mountains in the distance. He lived in a part of California that was rarely seen. Far to the north, near the Nevada border, the Pacific Rim's volcanic legacy was evident in the cone-shaped mountaintops, many of them dormant volcanoes, all of them in the distance.

He had to drop off supplies to one of his guests, an attorney from the Bay Area and a man Cabe didn't particularly care for. During yesterday's hunt all the man had cared about was "bagging the big one." He'd damn near shot another hunter in his eagerness. Thank God Cabe had stopped him in the nick of time.

"Just the man I wanted to see."

Cabe turned away from the bed of the John Deere Mule, a package of four-ply toilet paper in his arms, in time to spy the dark-haired attorney on the front porch of the cabin. All of the cabins had porches. All of them were made out of logs, too, the attorney—Stewart was his name—having called them *quaint* even though they were big enough to house a family of four.

"My toilet paper." The man reached for the bag of

four-ply Cabe had made a special trip into town to fetch. "Thanks."

"No problem." He was used to dealing with guests like Stewart, although they more frequently arrived with hunting season. They were men who were masters of their own universe back in town. They seemed to think that meant they could be in charge out in the wilderness, too, but they learned quickly that wasn't the case. Usually. Stewart had laughed when Cabe had told him he'd almost shot another hunter. That hadn't endeared him to Cabe at all.

"Anything else I can get you?"

Stewart smiled a greasy, oily smile that reminded Cabe of an infomercial salesman. "Yeah, the phone number of that blonde staying with you." He set the package of toilet paper down. "I hear she's single."

Cabe's jaw popped he clenched his teeth down so hard. "Yeah?" He rested his hands on his hips. "Who'd you hear that from?"

"Your daughter."

He would have to have a little talk with Rana about revealing information to their guests. "I think she's seeing someone."

Me.

The ridiculousness of the thought sent his mood plummeting even further.

"Yeah? Any way to find out for sure?"

It was rare for Cabe to dislike a guest this much, but he'd really started to despise Stewart and his pushy ways. The man probably thought a woman like Saedra would jump at the chance to date a big-time attorney from the city. Then again, maybe he should give the guy Saedra's number anyway. He'd learn for himself that she wasn't into city slickers.

Chapter Six

She took a step back.

He looked ready to grab the snow globe she'd unearthed earlier and throw it at her.

"I know you said not to decorate, but Rana and I..."

He took a step toward her. She glanced toward the stairs, wondering if Rana was around still, but all she heard was the sound of her own breathing.

"Rana misses Christmas." She held up her hands. "She told me that."

"This isn't Rana's house."

She took another step, her back coming into the contact with the door frame leading into the kitchen. "Yes, it is."

"This is *my* house."

"And Alana's getting married in it next week. It needed to be done. Otherwise, people would think it strange."

He took another step. They were inches away from each other now, and Saedra could smell the outdoors on him, wood smoke, hay and sweat. And though she would have never thought it possible, somehow, strangely, *crazily,* she found the angry, confrontational Cabe wildly and, yes, inappropriately attractive.

He finds you attractive, too. You know that. Don't let him scare you off.

"I don't give a crap what other people think." He leaned closer. "And neither should you."

She licked her lips. She saw his gaze dart down, saw his pupils flare, felt the heat from his gaze beam into her own cheeks. Frustration. Anger. Desire. Those were the headlines on his face today.

"I don't care." She pasted a brave smile on her face. "I just want things to look perfect for Trent and Alana." She licked her lips again. He once again followed the motion with his eyes. "Don't you care, too?"

"Of course I care about that."

"Then let it go," she told him, though she had no idea if she meant let go of his grievance against Christmas or let go of his own desire.

"I can't."

She took a deep breath, knew she was about to do something crazy, but she didn't care. "Yes, you can." She touched the side of his face.

She expected him to pull back. He didn't. Instead, he looked away for a moment, and it seemed that the shoulders beneath his denim shirt slumped as he all but growled, "What are you doing to me?"

She felt the breath leave him. "I'm helping you to live again."

He still wouldn't look at her. Her hand drifted down his cheek, and when he didn't pull away she leaned up on her tiptoes, brushed her lips against his own, a part of her horrified by her audacity, another part of her completely and utterly certain it was the right thing to do.

But you hate the man.

Apparently, that wasn't true.

"Kiss me," she whispered against his lips, tired of waiting for him.

He drew back a bit. She thought she'd lost him then, but suddenly he jerked her to him and kissed her. Hard. She moaned, though not in protest. Oh, no. Everything inside her leaped to life. Something hot slipped between her lips—his tongue—and the realization made her groan again because it titillated her insides in a way that curled her toes.

He tasted unlike anything she expected. A combination of sugar and cream and caramel. When he backed her up against the door, she didn't mind, and when he deepened his kiss, his tongue swirling around her own, she grew dizzy with need.

"Daddy?"

They jerked apart like two kids. Her cheeks turned as red as church bricks when Rana came around the corner, the teenager spotting them in the hall.

"Well?" the girl asked. "What do you think?"

Was he having as much difficulty regaining his equilibrium as she was?

"Oh, yes. I liked it."

But he wasn't talking about the Christmas decoration. Oh, no. Rana, however, was clueless. She rushed forward, giving her dad a hug.

"I *knew* you wouldn't be mad. I knew you'd understand. Doesn't it look great?"

The teenager had no clue. Even now they each took harsh breaths, Saedra's body warm in places that hadn't been heated by a man's touch in what felt like years.

"Looks beautiful."

Saedra blushed all over again. The heat in his gaze… it was still there, his eyes fixating on her lips for a moment in such a way that Saedra knew he was recalling the explosive moment of their kiss.

"So we can keep them up?"

Saedra tensed.

"For now."

At least it wasn't a no. If kissing him meant he would agree to things more often, maybe she should kiss him every day.

No, you shouldn't.

"Since you didn't freak out over the decorations, does that mean you can take Saedra and me into Reno tomorrow to go look at tents for the wedding?"

"What?" Saedra said. "Oh, no. There's no need for that. You and I can drive down by myself."

"But my dad can help us decide. Plus, he's been to Reno about a million times. He'll find the place way faster than you."

The teenager looked between the two of them, and Saedra would swear the teenager had picked up on the undercurrents sparking. Did she suspect? Were Saedra's lips red? Did she have that "just kissed" look about her? Was the girl old enough to even know what hanky-panky was?

She was.

Because when Cabe said, "That might be a possibility," she could have sworn the girl's eyes brightened.

"Really? Perfect."

No. It wasn't perfect. The only reason the man had agreed was because of what had just happened. Rather than scare him off, their kiss had done the exact opposite—not that she'd been trying to scare him off. Oh, no. She'd been curious what would happen; only now that she knew, she wondered what she'd gotten herself into. Gone was the Grinch. In his place stood a man who stared at her in frank appraisal, as if wondering just how far things might have gone if they hadn't been interrupted, a man who looked committed to finding out.

Lord help her, she wanted to find out, too.

SHE'D TIPPED HIS world on its axis.

It proved impossible to concentrate for the rest of the day. Cabe told himself it was because of the Christmas decorations, the sight of them keeping him from the house.

That's what he told himself.

The painful truth was that it wasn't just the decorations—it was that damn kiss, too. He'd been angry. Furious with her. That's why he'd done it. That's why he'd kissed her, but he knew that wasn't the truth. As much as it pained him to admit it, he'd wanted her—badly. Like a man fresh off a stint in the military, one who hadn't had shore leave in years, he'd been unable to stop himself from pushing her up against the wall, from taking his fill of her and from wishing they hadn't been interrupted. It had prompted him to agree to take her to Reno, something he knew he shouldn't do because what he should be doing was avoiding her at all costs. Thank God his daughter would be with them. Maybe then he'd be able to keep his hands off her.

He missed dinner that evening. Rana didn't complain. He waited until well after bedtime before returning, the house quiet, although he noticed the garland around the railing had tiny Christmas lights wound into it, making Cabe pause for a minute by the front door. At least there was no tree. He put his foot down at getting a tree.

Brrr eow.

The sound drew him up short.

Brrr oww.

He about jumped out of his shoes when something butted up against him, something soft and fuzzy and that he could now hear purring.

Son of a—

"What the hell are you doing down here?"

Rosey or Riley or whatever the darn cat's name was stared up at him unblinkingly, then it wound its way between his legs, brushing up against his jeans while staring up at him as if fully expecting Cabe to deposit a can of cat food at its feet.

"Yeah, good luck with that." He looked around, wondering if Saedra was nearby, or if maybe she'd let the cat out of her room while she worked downstairs. She was nowhere in sight, thankfully, or maybe not so thankfully.

He took the steps two at a time, the light from the banister railing illuminating the way. He opened Rana's door without even knocking.

"Saedra's cat is out," he announced. "You need to come get it and put it back in her room."

He flicked the light on overhead, and a bleary-eyed Rana pushed herself up on her elbows. "Whaaaaa?"

"Saedra's damn cat got out." He pointed with a thumb behind him. "Go put it back in her room."

"No." She lay back down and pulled the covers over her head.

Her defiance left him speechless for a moment. "Rana, I mean it. Go get it."

All he heard was a muffled, "You do it."

He stood there and, when she didn't move, knew he fought a losing battle. A teenager just out of REM was like a bear out of hibernation. Some battles weren't worth fighting.

Damn.

He turned away from the door, only to nearly stumble over the cat, who must have followed him up the stairs.

"Brr eow?"

"Don't meow me, cat," he told it. He could either leave the cat loose in the house or bring it up to Saedra's room.

He didn't want to go to her room.

The thought of opening her door knowing she was inside, asleep, in her nightgown, or maybe even naked—yipes—all alone, Rana in her own bed sound asleep, and that they could maybe pick up where they left off…

He bent and picked the thing up, holding it out from him. Ugliest cat he'd ever seen with its pushed-in face and piglike nose and fluffy gray fur. He would put it in his room for the night. But the moment he pulled it into his arms the darn thing tried to crawl right out. Actually, it tried to crawl up the front of his shirt, its claws like miniature grappling hooks.

"Ouch. Stop." He clutched it by the middle again and held it out from him. "What the heck, cat?"

The cat gave him a look that clearly indicated if Cabe had been a mouse, it would have bitten his head off.

"Yeah? The feeling's mutual."

He really didn't want to sleep with the darn thing. Maybe he should just let it run loose in the house, but he knew what cats were like. His house would be in shambles by the morning—it was one of the reasons he hated cats.

"To hell with it."

Up the third flight of steps he bounded, the Christmas light from below shedding a soft glow on the steps. He never even paused, just pushed open the door and tossed the cat inside.

"Hey!" Saedra cried, and she sounded perturbed.

He slammed the door closed. Given that he'd just tossed her cat into her room, he could understand why. He made it to the top of the landing.

"What were you doing with my cat?"

Not naked. She wore an oversize T-shirt, her shapely legs bare...and tan.

"I wasn't doing anything with it. Damn thing was downstairs."

There was just enough light that he could make out the expression on her face, one of confusion and bemusement. "He was out?"

All he could do was nod, those legs of hers driving him to distraction. And the way her hair fell over her shoulders, too, so long and pretty. And the outline of her breasts, which he could just make out...

Stop.

"Thanks for bringing him upstairs."

He nodded again, turned away, dismayed to realize the overpowering need to kiss her again was back again. What the hell was it with her?

"Cabe, wait."

No. Don't wait. Run like hell.

He paused, but didn't turn around.

"About this afternoon—"

"It was nothing," he called over his shoulder.

Was that footsteps? She hadn't followed him. Not in that skimpy T-shirt and what he fantasized were frilly underwear beneath.

"Cabe, it wasn't nothing."

She touched his shoulder. He flinched. She came up alongside of him.

"It's okay to feel physical attraction." She touched his hand, her fingers entwining with his own. "Especially when it's been so long."

Do not turn and face her. Do not.

"You're human." She tugged on his hand. "So am I."

She wasn't saying what he thought she was saying.

They barely knew each other. She was here to plan a wedding, not jump into bed with him.

"I have needs, too," she said softly.

He shouldn't. He really shouldn't, but when she tugged him toward her room, he knew he would.

Chapter Seven

What was she doing?

Whatever it was, a part of her didn't care. Like she'd said, they were two consenting adults, and there was nothing wrong with bringing pleasure to a man who needed a woman's touch more than any man she'd ever known. Besides, she had no idea how Ramses had gotten out of her room, and she took it as a sign that he was here, now, and they were alone.

The door opened on silent hinges, but he paused just inside the doorway, prompting her to glance back, the smile that'd been building on her face fading.

"What is it?"

He glanced around. "This was her room." He shook his head a bit. "Her office."

Her smiled faded even further. "I'm so sorry." She squeezed his hand. "I know what it's like to lose someone you love."

She moved in closer to him, looked into his eyes, tried to make him see that she did understand, and that it was okay to move on, okay to feel things again.

"What am I doing?" he mumbled.

She touched his cheek. He had such soft skin for a man. It was dotted with razor stubble, but not a lot, just enough that she could feel where it ended and smooth flesh began.

"You're acting on an instinct as old as the hills." Her smile returned. "So why don't you kiss me before I change my mind."

In case he needed further encouragement she grabbed the front of his denim shirt and tugged him toward her. He took one last look around the room. She lifted a hand, buried her fingers in the brown hair at the nape of his neck, urged his head down. When his gaze connected with her own she knew she'd won.

"This is crazy," he whispered.

Yes, crazy, she admitted just before their lips connected. Crazy and yet somehow right. They'd been at each other's throats since the day they met, but when they touched each other it all faded away.

His hands moved to her hips, jerking her up against him at the same time their lips connected. It wasn't a harsh kiss like it was before. No. His lips were surprisingly gentle as they caressed her own. Too gentle. She didn't want a gentle seduction. She wanted the man she'd kissed downstairs, the man driven to the edge of sanity, the man who'd been ready to have her up against the door.

She swung him around and pushed.

"Hey," he cried as he sailed backward.

He landed on the bed with a squeak of the mattress springs and a gasp of surprise that Saedra worried might have awoken Rana. She didn't give him time to change his mind, crawling onto his lap, his blue eyes widening just before she bent and kissed him.

Any doubt that he was as affected by her touch as she was his vanished the moment she felt the rock-hard swelling between her thighs. It gave her the courage to cup his face as she kissed him, to pressure him into opening his mouth, to shift her weight so that he sank back on the bed. This was how she wanted him, prone, helpless to do anything other than kiss her back.

And kiss her he did.

He opened his mouth wider, Saedra tasting him once again, his moist heat causing fire to slide down her body, pooling in places that hadn't been touched by desire's hot fingers in what seemed like ages. That he hadn't done this in just as long turned her on nearly as much as kissing him did.

She slid a hand between them, tugging at his waistband, her fingers sliding beneath and finding the deep ridges that surrounded all six of his abdomen muscles. The man worked hard for a living and it showed, the feel of his hard flesh even more of a turn-on than his kiss—if that made sense.

He flipped her on her back.

It happened so suddenly that she let out a squeal of surprise. She heard him laugh—really laugh—and Saedra's own spirits soared in response. A moon that had been full just a few days before brought bright light into the room, enough so that she could see the way his eyes crinkled at the corners, and the way they burned into her own, too.

"You sure about this?" He rolled off to the side as he waited for her to answer.

Something big and furry jumped onto her chest.

"Ramses!"

The cat ignored her cry of protest, his paws pumping into her belly, but only for a second because in the next instant he faced Cabe...and hissed.

"Hey!" Cabe sat up so quickly he nearly clocked her in the nose with his elbow.

"Ramses!"

Her precious feline reared back, claws extended. Cabe

yelled. Ramses swiped. Saedra yelled. Ramses took one look at her angry face and used her belly as a launching pad.

"Ouch," Saedra cried, clutching her belly. "Ouch, ouch, ouch."

"Are you okay?"

"I'm fine." They were both sitting up now, even Ramses, the feline having retreated to the corner of her room, back hair fluffed, eyes narrowed, tail flicking. "I might end up making a fur coat out of a certain feline, but I'm fine."

"Let me see."

She pulled her shirt out of her waistband, the mood in the room so completely different from only seconds before that she was half tempted to laugh.

Good job, Ramses.

"Ouch," Cabe said when he spotted the welts even moonlight couldn't hide.

"Dad!"

Cabe shot off the bed like a man caught cheating on his wife. Ramses began to howl. Cabe eyed the animal like a lion tamer with a chair.

Saedra laughed.

She couldn't help it. How had things gone from bad to worse in such a short amount of time?

"Dad?" Rana yelled again.

"I'm up here, honey."

He was trying to tuck his shirt into his waistband and looking for all the world like a man with ants in his pants. They both heard footsteps on the stairs. Cabe lunged for the door, swung it wide.

"In Saedra's room," he added—as if the girl hadn't already figured that out.

"I thought I heard someone yell," Rana said. Though it

was darker out on the landing, she could see Rana's concerned face when she stopped near the doorway. "What happened?"

Cabe glanced from his daughter to Saedra to the cat in the corner—still howling—then back to his daughter again.

"The cat got out, remember?" He scrubbed a hand down his cheek. "I asked you to help me put it back in Saedra's room, but you were out cold, so I had to do it, and cats and I don't mix, you know that. The damn thing attacked Saedra it was so mad at me."

"He didn't attack me," Saedra said before slipping out of bed and padding barefooted to Ramses. She scooped him up. "He was just upset about you…" *Touching me.* She knew Cabe heard the unspoken words, and Saedra bit back a smile. "About being manhandled."

The cat hissed in his direction. "See."

Rana laughed. "Ramses must have figured out my dad hates cats."

"I don't actually hate them, but whatever. Show's over." Cabe moved to Rana's side. "Let's leave Saedra alone now."

No. Don't go, she implored him with her eyes.

He ignored her.

Come back later.

But all he did was close the door. Saedra collapsed against the headboard, letting out a silent oath of frustration. Ramses jumped into her lap. She soothed the cat—although a part of her was tempted to throttle him. It'd been so long since she'd had a man in her bed. Who had time while training for the NFR, although to be honest, she really didn't like long-term relationships. They always ended badly. She'd learned the hard way men couldn't be trusted, which was why she preferred the love-'em-and-leave-'em type. Cabe was just her style. Damaged enough not to read anything into sex. Desperate enough to jump her.

Only he didn't.

After an hour or so, sleep began to tug at her eyelids, a keen sense of disappointment causing her to roll onto her side, making Ramses jump off the bed in irritation.

The man was a big old scaredy pants, that's what he was. She should forget about him. With everything she had on her plate, the last thing she needed was an affair with someone who didn't want her.

Except he *did* want her. She'd seen the longing in his eyes. She'd spotted the uncertainty, too, and the desire to feel like a man again. How long had it been for him? A year? Two?

He needed her. She wanted him, too.

She would just have to convince him of that fact.

HE SHOULD BE ashamed of himself, Cabe thought the next morning for about the thousandth time.

He wasn't the type of man to jump a woman simply because she was there. Now he would be forced to spend the whole afternoon in her company, all the while pretending last night hadn't happened, even as a part of him wanted it to happen again.

"Damn, foolish situation."

"You okay, Daddy?"

They were out checking the watering troughs, Rana along for the ride. She sat in the John Deere Mule while he scanned a four-by-two-foot concrete trough to ensure the automatic filling nozzle wasn't blocked or iced over or that the trough wasn't filled with mud or grass or a dead rodent. He'd seen it all over the years.

"Fine," he said, using the old coffee can he'd brought

along to scoop out debris. Fortunately, the storm that had blown through the other day had been a warm one, and the weather this morning was nothing short of perfect. It should have put him in a good mood.

It didn't.

"You don't look fine. You've been quiet the whole time we've been out here."

"Out here" was in the back pasture, a place so far away they'd climbed in elevation so that the ranch was off in the distance, a tiny speck of civilization amid green pastures. In the distance the volcanic mountains that surrounded them had received a fresh coat of snow, the tops of the peaks so white they almost seemed to glow.

"Just a lot on my mind, what with this wedding next weekend and our guests." Thank God he'd hired one of the local guys to take Stewart-the-know-it-all-attorney out today. In a couple of days the man would be leaving. So would their other guest, just in time for new guests to start arriving for the wedding.

Never ending.

"Are you in a bad mood because I interrupted your kiss?"

He about dropped the coffee can. "What?"

"And don't think for a minute I buy that story about returning Ramses. You were doing more than that."

"No, I wasn't."

"Dad. Don't lie."

Why did he suddenly feel like a kid caught with a girlie magazine. "I'm not lying. We weren't doing anything."

Not when you walked in. Not anymore at least.

His daughter seemed to read his mind, her long brown hair falling over one shoulder. She wore her black hat, the brim flat and wide, a fluffy down jacket hugging her tiny frame. He remembered a time when her feet couldn't reach the floorboard of the Mule, but now she sat in her seat, basking in the morning sun, a smirk on her face as she eyed her dad who was, yes, all right, *lying.*

"Your shirt was hanging out of the back of your pants."

He'd gone back to his task of scooping out debris, but her words made him look up again. "Must have come out when I was working."

"Yeah, right."

What did she want from him? It was bad enough that she'd convinced Saedra to decorate the house. Now she was hounding him about the woman.

"You like her, don't you?"

His face turned as red as the Radio Flyer wagon he'd gotten her when she was five years old. "She's not my type."

Rana slipped out of her seat. There were more cans in the trucklike bed of the four-wheel-drive vehicle. She picked one up.

"It's okay if you like her, Daddy. I don't mind."

No. Of course she wouldn't mind. His daughter was so sweet she would love anybody Cabe brought home. He was the one who minded. Saedra made him feel things, things he didn't want to feel. Not yet. It was too soon.

"I think she'd make you a good girlfriend."

He studied the water trough. No more debris. He set the can aside, the rim clinking against the concrete edge. "No. She would not make a good girlfriend."

She'd make a helluva one-night stand, though.

His face heated again, and his daughter's raised brows prompted him to say, "After the wedding she'll be off to Colorado, then out on the road barrel racing. She sold her business back home so she could do exactly that. She's not going to want a boyfriend. Not now."

"So you admit you *have* been thinking about it?"

"No." He hated lying to his little girl, but she needed to get these foolish thoughts out of her head. "I'm just relaying what Alana told me."

You're gonna burn in hell if you keep fibbing to your daughter like you are.

"She likes you."

He picked up the can again, brushing by his daughter so he could return it to the back of the ATV.

"You're confusing friendliness with something else."

She faced him again, crossing her arms when he motioned for her to get back in the Mule. "She gets all sparkly-eyed when she's around you, Dad."

"That's called irritation." He climbed into the passenger seat. "We rub each other the wrong way."

She still stood by the water trough, arms crossed. "You're going to take her out to dinner tonight."

"What, no—"

"I'm not going to go with you to Reno. The two of you will go alone."

"Rana—"

"And if you don't I'll let Ramses out of her room again to terrorize the house."

"What? You did that?"

"I knew you'd put him back in, and it seemed to me you needed a little nudge in Saedra's direction."

That his fourteen-year-old daughter had orchestrated his get-together with Saedra last night shocked him to the core. She wasn't old enough to do that, was she?

Apparently, she was.

"Take her out, Dad. You'll have fun."

He started the Mule, the engine chugging to life, the machine lurching as he put it in gear. He refused to be forced into doing something he didn't want to do, especially by his fourteen-year-old daughter.

She came forward, slowly sat next to him, giving him the same look she'd used on him when she wanted a sparkly new bridle or the latest and greatest bit for her horse.

"Come on." She smiled. "Who says she has to be your girlfriend. Go on out. Blow off some steam."

Wait. Was she implying what he thought she was implying?

She was.

He saw the way she wiggled her brows, the smirk she gave him, the visual equivalent of a wink and a nudge.

"You are something else."

She reached out, patted his hand. "I just want you to be happy again."

She wasn't a little girl anymore. The realization had struck before, but it really hit him over the head in that moment.

"I'll think about it."

"Goody."

"But if I ask her to dinner, and she says no, will you drop the matter?"

Her smile was as bright as the snowcapped mountains. "Deal."

Chapter Eight

"You want to do *what?*"

Saedra tried to keep her surprise to herself and she stared into Cabe's eyes, his black hat so low on his head it was almost hard to see them.

"Go to dinner when we're in Reno." He looked at the floor, the ceiling, the desk she sat behind, the window to her left—anywhere but at her. "Rana said she wants to stay here so it'd be just you and me."

After all but running away from her last night?

Oh, how she wanted to say exactly that, but his daughter stood next to him, the girl nodding her head and smiling.

They'd just returned from outside, Saedra having spent the morning immersed in work. She now had someone who could supply the tri-tips and ribs she planned to barbecue for Alana and Trent's wedding dinner. She'd decided on a wedding favor that was as unique as it was appropriate, too—horseshoes someone had cleverly crafted into a picture frame—inexpensive and yet cool. All in all, she'd been feeling very pleased with herself even as she wondered what would happen when she and Cabe were once again face-to-face. Now she knew. But to ask her to dinner...

"Okay, fine."

She saw him twitch, as if that wasn't the answer he'd been expecting, and then glance at Rana, who now beamed.

"Awesome," the teenager said.

She hooked Cabe's gaze with her own. "When do we leave?"

"Right now, if you want. It's going to take us a couple hours to get there."

Hours in a truck alone with him. This ought to be interesting.

"Great. I'll go get my coat."

He gulped, his Adam's apple bulging in response, and she almost smiled. So that's the way the wind blew? Clearly he hadn't wanted to take her out to dinner. The whole thing had been Rana's idea, and he'd been hoping she'd say no, only she hadn't—and now he was stuck.

Hah.

She had to fight to keep from grinning. She had no idea why she wanted to get under his skin, but she did. Actually, she wanted more than that, and since she was the type of woman to go after what she wanted, she saw no reason not to continue her mission to bring Cabe back to the land of the living.

"I'll be right back," she added, closing down her laptop with a smile. She ruffled Rana's hair on her way out the door, the teenager's smile indicating how pleased she was that her plan had come to fruition.

Ramses greeted her with a howl of protest.

"I know, I know." She bent to stroke the cat's head. "I know it's a pain in the rear to be cooped up all day, but it's the way it's got to be."

She wished she knew how he'd gotten out of the room yesterday. Rana had asked if she could play with him when she wasn't around. Maybe that's what had happened. Thank goodness Cabe had returned him before he'd slipped outside the house.

Though he might be a pain in the rear, the cat was the only steady relationship she'd had in the past few years. Sure she'd had the occasional date or two, but owning a business had meant she'd had little to no time to explore the opposite sex.

Maybe that's why she'd just about jumped Cabe yesterday. And maybe that's why she took time to change into a long-sleeved white shirt with gray stenciling and rhinestones. She brushed her hair, too, leaving it long and down her back. From her purse she retrieved a tube of lip gloss, mascara and, yes, even the blush.

Desperate, that's what you are.

The thought was enough to have her backing away from the mirror. She turned and scooped up her white down jacket, all the while calling herself a fool.

He didn't say a word when she reappeared, shrugging into her jacket on the way down the steps. He just headed for the front door.

Oookay. He was already to the driver's-side door of his truck when she paused on the front porch. This ought to be interesting.

When she climbed inside the vehicle it was like being shut inside a bank vault. Dead silence.

She cleared her throat, amped up the wattage of her smile. "So, how'd you sleep?"

He glanced at her sharply just before he started the truck, waiting for the engine to idle a second before saying, "Fine."

"Oh, yeah?" Her fingers beat a staccato rhythm on her thighs. "I didn't sleep a wink."

She felt him gaze at her again. Actually, now that she thought about it, this might be fun.

"Too bad."

"Yeah, too bad," she said. "Might have been a good night if someone hadn't been scared off by a cat."

He was right in the middle of putting the truck in gear, the transmission grinding for a moment, and Saedra's smile tried to break free. She wouldn't let it.

"That was for the best."

He finally got the truck in gear, and he gunned the engine so they were practically flying down the gravel driveway. They were past the house and his front pasture before she could say how-do.

A little hot under the collar, was he? Served him right. Coward.

"I guess that means you're the love-'em-and-leave-'em type."

He didn't say anything.

"You know, there's a word for that." Still no response. "Tease."

She might as well attempt a conversation with the Lincoln Memorial. She wondered if she should push him a little more, maybe see how far she could go, but decided against it. When they entered town, she wondered how long he'd keep it up, this silent routine. He couldn't be quiet the whole two hours, could he?

He slowed down. She assumed he must have to fill the gas tank because, when she looked up, they were still in town. No gas station, though. No. He was turning into...

A hotel. Well, a motel, really. "What are you doing?"

He still didn't answer.

"If you're trying to scare me, it won't work."

He pointed the truck into a parking spot in front of a room. It was one of those single-story places, the kind of motel that could be surprisingly nice inside, or not so nice; it was hard to tell with its adobe exterior and cactus landscape, although the quality of vehicles parked outside spoke in its favor.

He shut the engine off, turned to face her. "Time to put your money where your mouth is."

Now it was her turn to swallow. Hard. "What do you mean?"

One side of his mouth tipped up in what could only be called a smirk. Or maybe a smug look of anticipation. It was hard to tell which.

"I wasn't going to jump you last night with my daughter a stone's throw away.

"It sure seemed that way."

"Maybe at first, but then I changed my mind."

"I see."

"But I'm going to jump you now."

His words might have been a live wire they affected the hairs on her arm so much. "Really?"

He nodded. "But I want you to know, it doesn't mean anything. This…thing between you and me. It's just to blow off steam."

She leaned back in her seat. No doubt he believed what he was saying so he could remain guilt-free in honoring his marriage vows. Poor man didn't seem to realize his wife was dead.

"What makes you think I want more than sex?"

He stared her down. She held his gaze.

"Most women do."

"Not me." He didn't need to know about her past. Didn't need to know the number of times her heart had been broken. How she had *horrible* taste in men, a lesson she'd learned the hard way over the years. Easier just to use 'em and lose 'em, that's what she said. "I'm just in it for a good time." Just like most men.

Not this one.

She ignored the voice of reason because he was in it for the sex. That was all. The man didn't even like her.

She watched as his mouth lifted into a mirthless smile. "Good. Then I'll go get a room."

HIS HANDS SHOOK.

It'd been years. Absolutely *years* since he'd been with a woman. Frankly, he wasn't certain he could do it. Well, he could do "it." His hesitation was more a matter of whether he could actually go through with renting a room. As he handed over his license and a credit card his face blushed scarlet. The clerk behind the counter handed him a room key—an actual metal key, not the plastic card thing—and he could swear she smirked.

"Out the door and to the right. It's the second room."

She knows what you're up to.

No, he told himself, thanking her, she did not. He and Saedra could be tourists. They could be newlyweds. A couple of people visiting family in the area.

When he pushed through the door, frigid mountain air cooled his cheeks. He drew up short at the sight of Saedra leaning against the bumper of his truck, legs crossed, fluffy white jacket emphasizing her beautiful face. He'd never met someone so absolutely drop-dead gorgeous. Not since Kim—

No.

He would *not* think about Kim. Not today. He would think about Saedra and how much he needed what she offered. No strings attached. Just satisfying mutual need. Sex.

Move.

A smile broke out on Saedra's face as his footfalls echoed beneath a narrow overhang. Cabe had to admit that she had the sexiest mouth in the world. Plump. Dimples on each side. Soft skin. The memory of just how sweet she tasted ignited a lust such as he'd never felt before.

"You really did it."

He felt as if he'd run up a hill he was so out of breath. Her eyes, such a startling shade of blue they appeared almost neon, drifted over his frame, and suddenly it was as if he was struck by a million pricks of a needle.

"Let's go."

She didn't right away, though, just stared up at him for a second before pushing off. He heard her fall in behind him. His legs shook. His palms began to sweat. Fortunately, their room was almost directly in front of where they'd parked; otherwise, he didn't think he would have made it. He almost collapsed against the door, driving the key home with more force than necessary, then all but slamming open the door. He caught it from swinging wide just in time.

"Not bad," she said as she strolled past him. Cinnamon and vanilla. The scent assaulted his senses. Everything about her affected him. She was like a drug that had been tailor-made for his blood type.

He tossed the key on a Formica table to his left. She paused at the foot of the king-size bed that dominated the room, turned to face him and then slowly, ever so slowly, began to unzip her jacket.

Oh, man.

His body reacted instantaneously. He felt himself swallow, watched as she shrugged out of her jacket.

He couldn't move.

Her hands moved to her waistline. He briefly registered that her shirt had gray swirls and rhinestones on it and that it hugged her every curve. She never looked away as she tugged the thing slowly upward, exposing first the flat surface of her belly, then her rib cage, then the underwire of a bra that pushed her breasts upward.

He wanted to cup those breasts.

What are you doing?

The words were a shrill cry in his head. He blinked for a second. He was getting laid, he silently answered. By God. He would have sex with this woman because if he didn't, he would surely explode. He'd begun to throb, blood pooling near his center, his erection pressing against his zipper.

When she tugged the shirt over her head, her hair rose with it, but only for a second, the silky strands falling free in a glorious mass of golden hair. She reached behind her next, her striptease the most erotic thing he'd ever seen, and when she released the catches of her bra, the thing falling to the floor, her breasts springing free, he groaned.

Her fingers shifted to the snap of her jeans next; by the time she had them undone, blood was rushing through Cabe's ears in such a way that he knew he was a goner. He wouldn't be changing his mind. Oh, no. Instead, he watched her shimmy first one way, then the next, her fingers peeling the jeans slowly, ever so slowly, down, her underwear caught up with them, the vee near her thighs pale compared to the rest of her tan, smooth skin.

He throbbed.

Never, ever had he been so turned on by a woman. This was the sensual machinations of a seductress, a woman schooled in the art of pleasing a man, who wasn't ashamed of her body. When she straightened, her jeans flicked off to the side, she stood before him proudly, something close to a smile of satisfaction on her face.

"I'm going to have my way with you, Cabe Jensen. I hope that's okay."

Yes, he wanted to shout. It was great. Terrific. He wished she would hurry.

But she seemed to take pleasure in padding softly and slowly toward him. He didn't move, couldn't move, wondering what she would do. He had his answer a split second later when she stroked his manhood at the same time she jerked his head down to her own, her mouth already open when their lips connected, his groan of absolute and utter male satisfaction filling first his throat and then the room.

She stroked him.

He wasn't going to last. Damn it. The things she did to him...

She seemed to know that, her tongue diving into his mouth with the same rhythm as her hands, her body pressing up against his own, her tongue withdrawing at the same time her hands slid up the length of him.

His hips jerked.

She suckled him, lapped at his mouth, Cabe's body throbbing and pulsing and hardening and quickening and damn near exploding when her hand slid beneath the fabric of his jeans and cupped him.

He jerked his lips away.

"Saedra."

She clenched him.

"Don't."

She slid her fingers up his length.

"I'm not going to last."

She tilted her head back. "I know," she whispered.

He came. Hard. In her hand.

She laughed.

Chapter Nine

She had him right where she wanted him, she thought, giggling again. In the palm of her hand.

"Brat," she heard him whisper.

"It's been a long time, Cabe. I knew you wouldn't last." She flicked her tongue at his earlobe before capturing it between her teeth. She thought she heard him moan again as he jerked her hand out of his pants, then pushed her toward the bed. She fell willingly and, when she did, noted he was still hard.

Her seduction of him had completely turned her on. The slow striptease torture on her sensitive skin. His aloof regard a challenge she'd been unable to resist.

"Your turn to please me," she whispered before once again nibbling his ear, the hair of his sideburns tickling her nose.

He growled.

She smiled, wishing he was naked, her hands finding the waist of his jeans and unsnapping them. He didn't seem to mind. Not when she unzipped them, not when she started to tug them down, not even when she pulled his boxers over his hips. Yes, he was still hard. And slick. And she wanted. Oh, how she wanted.

"Protection?" he murmured in her ear.

"No need."

She was on the pill and he, well, he'd been celibate for so long she doubted there was anything to worry about. So when his hand slid between them, when he gently pushed against the inside of her thighs, she opened for him, silently begging him to take her...and take her now.

He did.

Hard.

She cried out. Did he laugh? A keening moan filled the room. Her own?

"Cabe."

His mouth found hers, and she realized she had gone from seductress to seduced. No. Taken. She felt him at her center. Time seeming to stand still as she waited...waited.

He plunged again.

She cried out, louder, her hands moving to his arms. So strong. So masculine. She didn't care that they were in a motel room. She could feel him, marveled at how taut his muscles were beneath her fingers, how good he smelled....

He thrust again.

She cried out, even more loudly. He withdrew, more quickly this time, and when he claimed her once again, she knew she was on the verge of a climax every bit as remarkable as his own. He drew back, stared down at her, his eyes never leaving her own.

Heartbreaking, she thought, what he'd been through. Sad. Nobody should have to go through—

He sank into her, more gently this time. Her groan turned into a sigh.

Her body welcomed him. Her heels found the backs of his thighs. She pulled him close, but he fought her efforts, pulled back again.

Yes.

She wanted this. Wanted this man. Wanted him inside

her. Hard or fast. Soft or slow. Harsh or easy. However he wanted to take her. As long as he took her. That was the turn-on, the thing that brought her higher, that took her one step closer, and that began to build and build until she just didn't think she could take it—

She climaxed, cried out, felt tears pool near the outer corners of her eyes. She blinked them away as she floated with the waves of her orgasm, gently drifting back to earth.

She felt him shift, hadn't known he'd been nibbling on her neck until suddenly she became aware of a stinging sensation where he might have bit her a little too hard. For some strange reason, when their eyes met, she felt overwhelmingly shy.

"Hi."

What a lame thing to say, she silently berated herself. The man had given her the first orgasm she'd had in forever and all she could say was hello?

"Hi," he said right back, smiling.

She relaxed because she'd never seen him smile at her the way he did right now. She felt him move, felt his hand find her head, his fingers moving through her hair as he bent and kissed her lightly on the lips.

"I hope you know I'm not done with you yet," she said.

"And I hope you know I'm not done with *you* yet."

Some things would never change, she realized, smiling. They would always have a spirit of competitiveness between them. It was just the way they were wired.

"Next time maybe we should take it slower." She reached up and stroked the side of his face, marveling at how soft his razor stubble was to touch.

"Next time maybe you shouldn't be so demanding."

She felt something build inside her, something that felt like laughter, but wasn't. Whatever it was, it made her stomach flutter, made her heart skip a beat, made her want to cry.

"How long has it been for you?"

He continued to stroke her hair. "You don't want to know."

"That long, huh?"

He kissed her, and Saedra's breath caught, her heart beginning to race. He kissed her so tenderly her stomach fluttered all over again, his lips soft against her own.

He drew back an instant later. "Long enough that I want to do it again."

She smiled. "Me, too."

HE COULD HAVE stayed in the hotel room all day, making love to her. It stank that they had to go to Reno, he thought as he reluctantly headed off to the shower.

"Wham, bam, thank you, ma'am," he heard Saedra murmur, but she shot him a smile as he disappeared behind the bathroom door.

Cold shower. That's what he needed. Otherwise, he'd be tempted to jump her again.

One afternoon wasn't enough.

As the cool stream of water peppered his face, he admitted he'd been fooling himself. One afternoon wouldn't be enough for him. Like the drug he'd equated her to earlier, he'd had a taste of her passion and he wanted more.

"Damn."

The shower drowned out the word, and Cabe leaned his head against the tile surface.

Now what?

"You going to stay in there all day?" he heard her call.

He shut off the taps. "Be right out."

A towel wrapped around his middle helped conceal the evidence of his desire. Who needed a little blue pill with someone like Saedra around, he thought, trying to act natural as she slid past him for her turn in the shower.

A half hour later they were back in the truck. Cabe felt like a teenage boy sneaking out of the girls' locker room, though he doubted anyone from town would recognize him, and they certainly wouldn't recognize her.

"Off we go," Saedra said as she climbed into the truck.

Fortunately, she appeared to like quiet as much as he did because they arrived in Reno having hardly spoken two words to each other, the radio off, the miles passing in a blur as he contemplated what to do from here on out. He finally managed to snap out of it as they approached their exit, but just in the nick of time. He almost missed it.

Selecting a tent to rent was accomplished with ease. They were lucky in one regard. Christmas Day wasn't a big day for really large parties. New Year's Eve was their biggest competition but everything fell into place. They even secured tables and chairs and, most important of all, a few massive portable heaters in case the day dawned cold. Heck, they even had the giant gas barbecues Saedra needed for the barbecue she planned to make.

Their next stop was a florist the rental shop recommended. To Saedra's delight they were only too happy to do a rush order, even offering to have the flowers trucked out with the wedding tent so that Saedra didn't have to make a trip into town.

"That was easy," Saedra said, the florist store's door tinkling as it closed.

Cabe opened the passenger's-side door, having a hard time keeping focus when he caught a whiff of her hair. Whatever shampoo she'd used in the shower, it smelled like honey, and he was man enough to admit he liked it.

"That only leaves hiring a pastor, the wedding license and a few other odds and ends."

She appeared very pleased with herself as he closed the door behind her.

He almost leaned against it.

The whole time she'd been arranging this and orchestrating that, he'd been unable to keep his eyes off her. Her bossiness might have bothered him before, but not anymore. He liked that she took charge. He loved that she wasn't afraid to tackle a problem head-on. Most of all, he was grateful that she'd put the moves on him earlier.

He wanted her to do it again. But he wouldn't let her because he'd only been blowing off steam with her. To touch her again meant he wanted more than a one-night stand, and that filled him with a sense of shame.

What would Kimberly think?

She would laugh at him. They'd always enjoyed an active sex life. Quite frankly he had loved touching his wife, but this wasn't his wife. This was a… He glanced over at Saedra as he started the truck. Just what was she to him, anyway? Certainly not a stranger. Not really a friend. Partner in crime? Was that a good way to think of her? Had it been a crime to have sex with her?

He scanned the rearview mirror, putting the truck in Reverse, and thinking he better keep his mind on driving before he did something stupid.

"You wanna try for another quickie?"

He slammed on the brakes.

She was all smiles as she said, "You paid for the room. Might as well put it to good use."

"We can't."

"Why not?"

He pulled back into the parking spot. "I'm not the type of guy that can use a woman for sex."

"Clearly, that's not true."

He winced. "I mean like you're suggesting." She

cocked a brow in question. "As in over and over again. I've never been that type of guy. Not even before..."

Kimberly.

But he didn't need to say her name. He read the understanding on her face.

"So this really was a one-time thing?"

"Yes."

He even nodded for emphasis, relieved she understood and that she wouldn't play the guilt card. Or suddenly profess her undying love for him. Or any number of scenarios he'd imagined during their drive south.

"How will we play it from here on out, then?" She tipped her head sideways, her eyes the color of a sapphire, gold hair spilling down one shoulder. His hand twitched he fought so hard not to reach out and touch it.

"Like nothing ever happened," he said. "That's how it's got to be."

She didn't seem upset by his words, not at all. In fact, she almost seemed relieved, too.

"Not a problem."

She reached toward her purse, pulling out the list he'd seen her consult over the past few hours.

"Let's see, I think I'll make some phone calls on our way back to the ranch. That'll help me out a bit. Will that bother you?"

That was it. Discussion over. No dramatics. No tearful admonition. No crazy theatrics. Now that they were done, it was business as usual.

"Won't bother me at all."

It bothered the hell out of him. Crazily, ridiculously, unbelievably, he felt *used.*

It wasn't a feeling he liked at all.

Chapter Ten

There was a surprise waiting for them at the ranch when she and Cabe pulled up a few hours later.

"Trent?" Saedra said when she spied the dark-haired man sitting on a bench on the Jensens' front porch. It was dark outside and so all she could make out was a broad-shouldered man and a smaller shadow next to him. "Alana?"

The two stood up.

"It *is* you!"

There was enough light from a nearby lamppost to spot their smiles as Trent and Alana got to their feet, the couple clasping hands and walking toward them, only letting go of each other as they gave their friends hugs.

"Man," Saedra said, "I can't tell you how good it is to see you up and walking."

Trent tipped his hat back, Saedra thinking to herself that he looked happy. "I can't tell you how good it *feels* to be up and walking."

He had a lot to be happy about. Her longtime friend had just won the average in team roping at the National Finals Rodeo and he would soon have a beautiful new wife, a woman as gorgeous on the inside as she was on the outside.

"You're back early." It was Cabe who'd spoken. "I'm sure Rana almost knocked you over when she saw you."

Alana nodded, and even in the near-darkness, Saedra could see her smile. "I think I just about knocked *her* over."

"Let's go inside." Saedra glanced at the sky. It was clear as a bell, a precursor to freezing temperatures Rana had told her about not too many days ago. "Speaking of Rana, where is she?"

"She's upstairs." Alana stepped up alongside her. "Something about wedding favors."

Oh, yeah. She'd put Rana in charge of printing out the photos of Alana and Trent that would go inside the horseshoe frame while Saedra was in charge of spray-painting the manzanita branches she planned to use for centerpieces.

"Did she show you what we're doing?" Saedra opened the front door, stepping back to allow her friends inside. Cabe glanced at her, the look he gave her the same one she'd caught on the ride back home.

What was with him?

"She did." Alana paused by the front door and shrugged out of her jacket. "I love the idea."

"Simple, charming and, most of all, easy to do in a short amount of time."

"I can't wait to see what else you've done." After she hung up her jacket, Alana clasped her forearm and leaned in next to her. "Knowing you, it's going to be fantastic."

"I hope so."

"Rana tells me things are going pretty well." It was Trent who spoke.

"They are." Saedra turned toward Cabe. "We just signed a contract for your wedding chapel." She smiled wryly. "Which is really a tent that looks like a miniature

Denver International Airport the roof is so strange. It's really cool, though."

They headed into the kitchen, Saedra wondering if Alana found it odd to be back. They'd only been in Colorado for a little over a week.

"Hey, how'd you like Trent's mom?" Saedra asked as they all sat down at the kitchen table.

"She's amazing."

Saedra nodded. She looked upon Gretchen Anderson as a second mom. Okay, really more like the mom she never had. Gretchen had been sure to love Alana—the woman who'd healed her son—and from everything she'd heard, Alana was certain to love Gretchen. She was so glad they'd all gotten along.

"Can't wait to see her next week." Saedra hopped up, grabbed some mugs down from the cabinet, the pot of coffee Cabe always seemed to have at the ready. "She's flying in on Sunday, right?"

The smell of coffee filled the room. Next week would be crazy, which was why she'd been so desperate to get the tent and flowers out of the way. The rest of the stuff was easy, but with guests arriving, Saedra would be running in twenty different directions.

"She is," Trent said, taking the mug she handed him. "Cheers."

The four of them sipped as they went over what they had planned. Saedra caught Cabe's gaze on her once or twice. Something was definitely up with him.

"Let's go upstairs and I'll show you what Rana's working on." Saedra picked up her mug. "You're going to love it."

"I'm going to stay down here," Trent said. "Gonna see if I can talk Cabe into selling me a horse."

Saedra nodded. He must mean Baylor.

"Yeah, good luck with that." Alana bent and kissed the top of her future husband's head. "I'll be right back."

They headed upstairs, but they hadn't even reached the bottom landing when Alana said, "Rana tells me you and Cabe went out to dinner."

For some reason, the words made Saedra blush. "No, ah…" She placed her hand on the railing, admiring the garland and the twinkling lights before saying, "We never made it."

Alana's nose seemed to wrinkle in amusement. "No?"

"No."

"But I take it the two of you are getting along."

If she only knew.

"Oh, yeah. Much better."

Saedra took the first step, but Alana didn't follow. "For real?" the brunette asked when Saedra glanced back.

"For real, Alana."

The woman she'd begun to look upon as a friend pulled her down onto a step next to her.

"The man was shooting you some seriously strange looks over coffee," Alana said.

It killed her not to ask Alana what she meant because Saedra would really love to get the other woman's opinion on just what, exactly, those looks were all about. She thought she'd made it pretty clear that all she'd wanted was a one-day fling. He'd said that was okay. Yet now she wasn't so certain. She could have sworn she'd seen irritation in his eyes. That, and confusion. Heck, maybe even defiance.

"He's just stressing about the wedding," Saedra said.

"I thought maybe it had something to do with the Christmas decorations."

She'd completely forgotten about Cabe's objections. "No. I don't think it's that."

Alana tipped her head sideways. "I couldn't believe it when I walked into the house."

Saedra glanced toward the kitchen, but they were far enough away that all she heard was the quiet murmur of Trent and Cabe talking.

"I thought he was going to pop a blood vessel when he saw what we'd done."

"I'm surprised he didn't demand you take everything down."

No. He'd kissed her instead.

The memory of that kiss, and the ones they'd shared today, made the muscles of her stomach ripple.

"It was…touch and go there for a while." That was one way of putting it. He'd touched her all right.

"But no tree?"

Saedra shook her head. "No. Rana didn't want to go that far."

"I'm not surprised."

"She wouldn't tell me why."

She heard Alana release a sigh, but it was one of sadness, not impatience.

"I assume it has something to do with his first wife," Saedra asked.

"Yes and no." Alana's nose wrinkled as if debating how much to tell her. "Did you know this house used to be a stagecoach stop?"

That seemed like an odd change of subject, but Saedra went with it. "No."

"Yup. The living room was the main parlor, the family room the dining room. The rooms upstairs were for travelers. The attic space was the maid's quarters."

"No kidding."

"No kidding," Alana said with a nod. "It's been in the Jensen family since forever. Cabe's great-great-great-something-or-other had it built. When the gold rush was over, the family had amassed enough land to start raising cattle."

She'd wondered how Cabe had acquired the ranch, although she'd assumed he'd inherited it. One didn't just "buy" a place like New Horizons Ranch.

"It was Cabe's great-great-great-grandmother that started the best tradition of all, at least in these parts. To hear Cabe tell it, she single-handedly started the trend of Christmas trees in California. The story goes one of her guests told her about Queen Victoria and how she had trees in her castle, and how the trend had caught on in England, and so nothing would do until Great-great-great-grandmother had her own tree. So she sent the menfolk up into the hills, had them drag the biggest Douglas fir they could find, tied ribbons and bows on it. Guess it was a really big deal. Things sort of took off from there."

"Wow. That's neat."

"I know." Alana smiled. "Or course, it's not in any of the history books, but there are enough old-timers around here who can corroborate the story that it's kind of an established fact that the Jensen family was the first to bring Christmas to this part of California. At least, Christmas as we know it. Kimberly, Cabe's first wife, carried on the tradition in a big way. She used to put the tree in front of the big picture window." Alana pointed. "Every year she'd have an annual Christmas tree celebration. It was a big deal around here before she died."

Well, no wonder, Saedra thought. No wonder he'd been in a strange mood, even after their little... Well, their time together.

"So consider it a major coup that he let you keep the decorations up. It couldn't have been easy to see all her things again."

"No. I guess not."

Alana took a deep breath. "So while I know he's been a pain in the rear, I hope you won't let it stop you from becoming friends."

She almost laughed. If only Alana knew. "I think we're well on our way to that."

"Good." Alana slapped her thigh. "'Cause he's not going to be happy when we force him to get a tree."

"What?"

"I think it's time, Saedra. He got over the decorations. He'll get over having a tree, too."

"I don't know…"

"I do." She stood. "It's a done deal. This weekend we're heading into the hills, whether Cabe likes it or not."

"Whether I like *what* or not?"

They both started, neither of them having heard him come out of the kitchen, although come to think of it, it'd gotten quiet. Where Trent had gone Saedra had no idea.

"Don't talk to me about it," Saedra said. "This is all Alana's idea."

"*What's* Alana's idea?" Cabe's gaze drifted between the two of them, the flashing Christmas lights and his narrowed gaze causing her to think of Halloween lights instead.

"We're going Christmas tree hunting this weekend," Alana announced.

Yup. Just as she suspected. Not happy. He didn't even have to open his mouth for Saedra to know that much.

"Trent and I were talking about it," Alana said. "It's time, Cabe, and we really want a Christmas theme for our wedding, but we can't do that without a tree."

Still nothing.

"I know you don't want to hear it, but when I saw all

the decorations, I couldn't have been happier. So please don't say no. This is something I believe all of us want."

Cabe's gaze fixed on Saedra. "Did you put her up to this?"

"No." Saedra lifted her hands. "I swear."

"She didn't. Ask Trent. He thinks it's a good idea, too."

Clearly, Cabe disagreed. Just as clearly, he hadn't absolved her of guilt. She recognized that look. It was the same one he'd had just before their first kiss. A silent promise.

She shivered.

Crazy enough, she couldn't wait.

Chapter Eleven

He wanted to say no to the tree, he really did, but for some reason he just couldn't do it, probably because of Alana's hopeful expression.

This was Saedra's doing. He was certain of it.

"Fine. Whatever." He turned away, so out of sorts he forgot what he'd come to tell them, but it came back to him almost instantly. "I need to go start the fire outside. We have guests coming up."

The last thing he felt like doing was socializing, but even in the winter, their bonfires were a part of the New Horizons experience. With any luck, nobody would show and he could call it an early night.

In Saedra's room. As long as she put away that damn cat. Beat the hell out of him why his daughter seemed to like it so much. That's all he'd heard about yesterday was how cool it was having a cat around. Hah. Rana clearly didn't know Ramses all that well.

As it turned out he wasn't so lucky. Within a half hour of starting the flames, Stewart and company showed up. There were times, albeit infrequently, when Cabe truly wished he did something different for a living.

"Howdy, pardner," Stewart announced in what Cabe suspected might be a John Wayne impersonation, one that failed miserably. "Haven't heard back from you about that pretty little filly of yours. Didya talk to her for me?"

Yeah. The man was trying to be funny but couldn't pull it off.

"Haven't had time." To be honest, with all the Christmas decoration hullabaloo, he'd completely forgotten to ask, not that he needed to. He knew what Saedra's response would be if he told her about Stewart's interest in her.

"Yeah?" Stewart's protruding nose looked more bulbous by the firelight.

Hey, now. You're just upset the man wants to ask Saedra out.

He was, damn it, and after the things they'd done together, he should be allowed to feel that way, too, except Saedra didn't want him. All Saedra wanted was sex, and most men would be happy with that. He realized too late he wasn't that type of man. Sharing her after being in bed with her... Nope. Didn't like it at all.

"She'll be out in a moment." Cabe pulled his flat black hat low down on his brow. Though it killed him to say it, he forced himself to say, "Why don't you ask her yourself?"

"I think I will." The man took a seat in one of six lodgepole chairs, ones with wooden stars decorating the back and arms, something that had cost Cabe a small fortune, but that a man like Stewart would consider "hillbilly," no doubt.

"Feels like it might snow."

"Yup." But they might need some precipitation for that to happen, he almost said sarcastically. The sky above could only be described as deep black, the ghostly ribbon of the Milky Way staining the sky.

"Is it always so cold here?"

His words were interrupted by the arrival of none other than Saedra, Rana and the happy couple themselves. He watched as the flickering firelight illuminated Stewart's gaze as it narrowed in on Saedra. Oh, he turned his gaze on Trent and Alana for a split second, his eyes skating over Alana's worn jeans and Trent's cowboy hat and instantly dismissing them—or so it seemed to Cabe.

"It feels like forever since I've sat in front of a bonfire," Alana said, sitting in one of the chairs and holding out her hands. "I've missed it."

"Stewart, this is my best friend, Alana, and her fiancé, Trent."

The man hardly spared them a glance. Okay, maybe he gave Alana a quick once-over, but his gaze returned almost immediately to Saedra.

"Trent here just won the average at the National Finals Rodeo in team roping."

"Oh, yeah?" Stewart asked, sounding about as interested as a man in the middle of doing a crossword puzzle.

"Saedra's going to win the average next year," Rana announced, taking a seat opposite Stewart. "In barrel racing. Aren't you, Saedra?"

"I'm sure going to try."

It took everything he had to keep what he felt off his face, especially when Stewart poured on the charm with a wide smile of his own.

"Is that a big deal or something?" he asked.

Rana snorted. "Ah, yeah. Didn't you see it on television?"

Stewart straightened. "They televise rodeos?"

"Are you kidding?" Rana said, and she didn't bother to hide her disdain. It wasn't like his daughter to be anything less than social to their guests. Clearly, Stewart was an exception. "They do it all the time, sometimes even on major networks, like ESPN."

No, Stewart was kidding, but just as clearly he'd never seen a live rodeo in his life, much less one on TV.

"Wow. I'd like to see you ride sometime," he told Saedra with a wide smile. "You must be pretty good if you think you can make it to the finals."

By firelight she looked even more stunning than usual in her off-white jacket, the one that framed her face. Stewart undoubtedly noticed, at least judging by the way he smiled.

"We don't do too bad." Saedra smiled, though it was clear she was only being polite.

Another one of their guests arrived, the owner of the dealership, an older man with gray hair and a wide smile and who'd been to the ranch every year they'd been open, and for the first time that night, Cabe wanted to smile.

"Glad to see some things never change." The man took a seat, glancing around the fire. "Alana! I heard you were off in Colorado."

"Mr. Edwards." Alana got up from her seat to give the man a hug. "So good to see you."

A few minutes later someone else joined them, a father and son visiting the ranch for the second time, the two of them all smiles thanks to the bighorn elk they'd brought down. The scene should have soothed his frayed nerves, but it didn't, Cabe's gaze sliding back to Saedra time and time again. She was laughing at something Stewart said, something about her cat, and just above the murmur of the crowd, Stewart's remark about how he loved kitties.

Right.

He'd had enough. Normally, he would hang out with his guests. Now would be a good time to catch up with Alana, find out how she liked Trent's mother, and what she thought of Saedra's wedding plans so far, but he didn't have the stomach for it.

"I'm headed to bed."

He glanced at Saedra and it was clear she hadn't heard him. Rana, however, had.

"Now?" she cried. Alana and Trent appeared just as startled.

"Tired. Big day ahead of me tomorrow. Taking a group of guests hunting in the morning."

"That includes me," Mr. Edwards said. "Guess I better turn in, too."

"Well, I'm staying out here," Rana announced.

He smiled his good-nights, trying hard not to catch Saedra's gaze, but doing it nonetheless. She frowned. He nodded and that was that. Escape. That's what he needed. Maybe if there was some distance between the two of them he could more easily forget their hours in bed together.

He headed straight for his bedroom, but on his way by the family room, his gaze caught on the snow globe with the carousel horse inside. Kimberly had loved it. She used to shake it every time she pulled it out of the box, smiling as she stared at the white pony with the golden saddle, turning it up and down a half dozen times, it seemed. He did the same, hardly realizing he'd moved toward it, much less picked it up. Inside the globe, tiny snowflakes swirled and danced and then gently settled back down.

"Do you miss her?"

He almost dropped the globe. Saedra gasped. He clutched it to him just in time.

"Gosh, Cabe, I'm sorry. I didn't mean to startle you."

"It's okay." He set the globe back down, then turned toward the stairwell. "Good night," he said as he passed by her.

"You didn't answer my question."

And he wouldn't.

"Cabe." She hooked his hand with her own, pulled him to a stop. She'd shed her jacket somewhere along the way, and so had he, the result being very little barrier between them, and he could feel the heat from her skin. "I'm sorry."

He hated that he noticed how warm she was. "About what?"

"It must feel like we're poking at an open wound." She shook her head. "First the decorations and now Alana insisting we get a tree."

He tried to pull away. She wouldn't let him.

"I'm sorry for that."

All he could think to say was, "Yeah," but it was hard to form the word, harder still to stand in front of her, to stare into her eyes, see the kindness and compassion in them.

"I need to get to bed."

She closed the distance between them, lifted a hand, and he knew what she was about to do.

"Saedra—"

She cupped the back of his head, and Cabe couldn't seem to stop himself from letting her draw his head down and from letting her soft lips caress his own. He allowed himself to forget for just a moment that she was right; it did hurt.

But she made that pain fade.

His hands lifted, his fingers sliding into her silky hair, his head tipping sideways so he could deepen the kiss. Touching her, tasting her, he could have gone on doing that—only that—for hours. She was so sweet, the insides of her mouth so hot, the feel of her tongue like a velvet ribbon, one that wound itself around his own and sent a jolt of awareness through his insides. It provoked a primal reaction, one that caused him to drop his hands and pull her hips up against him.

His fingers found the line of her jaw, then her neck, his tongue flicking out and following the same path as his hands. She groaned.

He lifted his head, sucked in a breath, knew if he didn't step back he'd push her down on the couch and land on top of her like a hormonal teenager.

"Saedra, we shouldn't."

She looked up at him, her eyes the color of storm clouds in the room's half-light.

"Yes, we should."

"There are guests outside."

"We can make it quick."

"I'm not worried about quick, I'm worried about quiet."

"I can be quiet."

He almost laughed.

She took his hand. "Come on. Everyone's outside."

She tried to lead him toward the stairs and, God help him, he followed. The snow globe. It was the damn snow globe. It had left a mark, those memories, marks he wanted to erase, and he knew she could help him do that.

She knew where his room was. He shouldn't be surprised. What did surprise him, however, was the way she gently led him to the bed, the way she paused for a moment to stare up at him. A light was on in his bathroom; it allowed him to study the emotions in her eyes. Sadness. Tenderness. And, yes, desire.

"Make love to me, Trent."

Amazing, the power of those words. Amazing what they did to him. Amazing that he could spend an afternoon in her company and be every bit as aroused the second time around.

He kissed her, and it was different this time. Earlier had been hot. Harsh. Urgent. This time it was soft, sweet, gentle. A simple kiss.

She drew back, nuzzled his lips with her own, then opened for him so that his tongue could slide inside her mouth. As he tasted her again, he admitted he'd never tasted anything quite so sweet. His hands moved up to her hair again, marveling at how thick it was. Her hands found the buttons on his shirt, began to pop them free one by one.

And all the while they kissed.

He would suckle. She would sip. He would nibble. She would nip. He would swipe. She would lick.

"What are you doing to me?" he heard himself ask.

"Helping you to forget."

She was, especially when her hands pushed his shirt off his shoulders, and it fell to the floor. She slowly slid down his jeans. Boots were kicked off…somewhere. Socks, who knew? Clothes strewn about the room. He didn't care.

"Touch me," she said, lifting his hand and placing it on her breast. "Please."

God help him, he did. She was heavy in his hands. He tested the weight, pressed his fingers into her. She groaned. He slid his other hand beneath her shirt, fingers sliding beneath her bra, finding her nipple, his head lowering so he could taste it and lap at it and lightly catch it with his lips.

"Cabe."

He felt her shift, her shirt suddenly disappearing. Her bra came off next, but it was all done slowly, and when she stood naked in front of him, long hair streaming down her back, blue eyes gazing intently into his own, he felt something shift. Like tumblers clicking into place, he admitted he desired this woman. Not just physically, but in other ways, too. Deep down he'd known that. It was why he'd been so rude to her when they first met. Why he'd stayed away. Why he came across as terse and, yes, as an ass.

Tonight, he lost the will to fight.

"Saedra," he said softly, gently, a touch of wonder in his voice that even he could hear. "You're a miracle, do you know that?"

"No, Cabe. You're the miracle. To love a woman so much." She reached up and touched him. "To mourn her for so long…" Were those tears in her eyes? "I can't imagine loving someone that much."

Couldn't she? Why not?

But then he forgot the question as she once again reached up and kissed him. They fell onto the bed, her body beneath him, and there was no petting or groping or foreplay. She opened for him instantly and he sank into her willingly, her sigh sending another jolt of…something through him.

"Saedra," he said again as he kissed her, his body gently taking what she so willingly offered. She was right. They could do it quietly, with soft whispers, hushed moans, gentle lovemaking. And as they both climbed higher and higher, Cabe felt himself let go…finally let go, tears filling his eyes as he buried his head in the crook of her neck and climaxed so exquisitely it was all he could do to keep on breathing.

"Cabe?" she whispered.

Had she climaxed, too? God, he didn't know. What kind of lover was he?

"Are you okay?"

He took a deep breath. "Fine."

She shifted a bit, and though he didn't want her to see him, she somehow managed to flip on her side so she could face him.

"You're crying."

"No."

He saw her face crumple, saw her lips begin to quiver, saw her own eyes fill with tears. "Oh, Cabe, it's okay."

He'd never cried in front of a woman in his life. Not even when they'd buried Kimberly. Not even when he'd been told Rana would never walk again. Not even when Rana had proven everyone wrong. But he felt a sob begin to build.

"Shh," she soothed.

He let it all go. Held her tight. And she let him. God bless her, she let him.

Chapter Twelve

She didn't want to leave him, but she knew she would have to. Rana could come upstairs at any moment. Alana might call out to her. Sure, she'd told everyone she was heading to bed, but one never knew.

He'd quieted down now, but Saedra's heart ached all over again. The look on Cabe's face…

"Cabe, I should probably get going."

He didn't answer, and when she turned to look at him she realized he'd fallen asleep. At peace now. Quiet. For a man who rarely stayed still for longer than two seconds it was odd to see him resting. Handsome. He had razor stubble on his chin, hair mussed, lips soft. She reached out and used the back of her index finger to stroke his sideburns. So soft. Like the man inside. He might come off as hard and indomitable, but inside he was anything but. And a good man, according to Alana. *The best,* according to his daughter. If she were any other type of woman she would snap him up.

She slid out from beneath the covers, suddenly uncomfortable with the direction of her thoughts.

Ramses scolded her the moment she entered her room. Cabe wouldn't approve of how she scooped the animal up and held him close. Her cat had never let her down. He was always there for her. He'd never taken her love and tossed it away like so many of the men in her life... including her own father.

Sleep was a long time coming. She kept expecting Cabe to slip into bed with her. He didn't. She heard Rana come in. Heard the house grow quiet again and then she fell asleep, but not for long. She woke before the sun came up only to lie awake for who knew how long, Ramses curled up next to her side. She finally gave up, dressed quickly in jeans and a fuzzy brown sweater, patted Ramses and said, "I'm sure Rana will keep you company again today," before turning and heading downstairs.

Cabe was there.

He sat at the kitchen table and stared out at a slowly brightening sky, his eyes squinting as he looked into the distance, jaw relaxed, face still covered in a day's growth of black razor stubble.

She almost turned around, but he must have sensed her stare because suddenly he faced her. She expected him to frown, maybe go back to what he'd been doing, but all he did was say, "How'd you sleep?"

She breathed a sigh of relief. "Good."

"I was about to get up and cook some breakfast. Want some?"

Not really. She felt...strange. Like the time she'd taken Dramamine and everything had gone all fuzzy around the edges.

"Sure," she said instead.

He got up and pulled a cast-iron skillet from a bottom cabinet. In minutes the smell of sizzling bacon caused her stomach to grumble. He didn't say anything as he cooked and she didn't encourage conversation. He just went about his business and she wondered, did he feel any different this morning? Had his breakdown in her arms helped? Why did it matter? That was the most troubling question of all.

"How do you like your eggs?"

"Over easy."

He shot her a smile and Saedra's insides turned to mush. Uh-oh.

"My kind of woman."

Moments later he placed two plates on the table, and Saedra thought she could get used to this, especially when he went back and poured her a mug of coffee.

"Cream? Sugar?"

"No, thanks."

Whoa there, cowgirl. You made a deal with yourself, remember? Love 'em and leave 'em.

In a week she'd be gone. Back home. Rodeo circuit full-time. Trying to make her dreams come true. That dream did not include a man, not even a handsome son-of-a-cuss who'd melted her heart with his tears. *Especially* not that kind of man. They were the most dangerous type. Needy. Clingy. Thoughtful…until they didn't need you anymore and then, wham, suddenly you were yesterday's dinner.

"Aren't you hungry?"

She hadn't touched her food, she realized. She instantly picked up her fork and dug in. Nothing like fried eggs and bacon for breakfast.

"Is this how you treat all your morning-after women?" she teased.

That's better. Keep it light. No pressure.

"Wouldn't know." He took a sip of his coffee. "Haven't been a whole helluva lot of women to treat."

No. Of course not. He'd married young, according to Alana. He and Kimberly had been high school sweethearts. She struggled to find something to say, something that would change the subject.

"What are your plans today?" She'd heard him out by the fire. He was going hunting. Probably why he was up so early.

"Did you enjoy yourself last night?"

For some strange reason the question—coming as it did from such a confident man—made her want to smile. "Of course I did."

"No." He took another sip of coffee. She wondered if he'd spiked it with something to give him courage. "*Enjoy* enjoy."

What was he...?

Understanding dawned. "Of course I did."

She could tell he still wasn't certain she understood.

"It was good for me, too, Cabe. Really good."

His face cleared. She had to look away, chastising herself for finding it so endearing that he was worried, really bothered by the fact that he'd hadn't been paying close enough attention to her to know for certain that he'd given her pleasure.

As if finally satisfied, he took a big bite of food. She realized the question had been weighing on his mind. Too cute.

"Sooo?" she prompted. "You going to go bag some big game?"

"That's the plan."

Comfortable. That was the best way to describe how sitting with him felt. Comfortable and nice. None of that awkward morning-after stuff that oftentimes happened.

"What about you?" he asked. "What are your plans?"

"Wedding dress shopping."

"Lucky you."

"I know. I can't wait."

He must have caught the sarcasm in her voice because he said, "I thought all women loved to go shopping."

"I'd rather be riding."

He scooped up the last of his eggs, Saedra thinking he'd all but inhaled the darn things.

If it walks like a man and talks like a man, it probably eats like a man.

Cabe Jensen was all man. Big boned. Broad shouldered. All muscle. She'd felt that for herself yesterday.

And yet softhearted, too.

"You really think you have a chance at making it to the NFR?"

"With my new horse, yes." She better have. She'd paid a small fortune for the animal. Too much money to get all gooey-eyed over a man and lose focus.

"Look." He pushed his plate away, but he didn't move, Saedra realizing he had something he wanted to get off his chest. "I know we promised to keep things casual, but I'm going to tell you right now, I'm not that kind of guy. Sex means something to me. I can't just…do it. It's personal, and I thought I was okay with what you said… at first. But now, after last night, I'm not. So if you want me to act all casual like, it's not going to happen. And I'm not going to pretend like there's nothing between us, either. I'm a cowboy. You're now my woman. Whether you like it or not, that's the deal. Get used to it."

He got up from the table, plate in hand, deposited it in the sink before coming back to her.

"Have a good day." He bent and kissed her on the cheek.

Saedra just sat there, stunned, as he left the kitchen. Only when he was gone did reality hit.

"Oh, dear."

HE TOLD HIMSELF to stay away from her for the rest of the day, something that was easy to do given he had guests to entertain, and a few of them leaving. By the time he returned later that evening, he fully expected to bump into her, but as it turned out, she was out with Alana and Trent. More "wedding" stuff, his daughter told him. He waited for her, but clearly she sought to avoid him because she hadn't made an appearance by that evening. Cabe was disconcerted to realize he didn't have her cell phone number. He called Alana instead and learned they had taken Saedra out to dinner and that Saedra had requested they go out afterward so that she could "scope out" the local male population.

A slap in the face.

That's how the words hit him. That was how she'd meant them. He'd issued a verbal challenge this morning. She'd thrown that challenge back at him.

She didn't know him that well.

The thing about a small town was that there were only a couple of places where one could grab a cold beer or a drink, and of those, only one of them that Alana actually liked. So after kissing Rana goodbye, he headed out, dressed in his best jeans and a blue button-down shirt, black cowboy hat firmly in place.

The bar was the same as a million other bars across the country. Bar to his left, vinyl-covered stools beneath it, wineglasses hanging upside down above. There were tables and chairs to his right, and a wooden floor at the far end of the building, where Saedra danced.

With Stewart.

Cabe stopped in the doorway, everything inside of him seeming to still for a second, before erupting into a riotous cacophony. Country music played from hidden speakers. It seemed too loud to him all of a sudden. The voices coming from the bar too jumbled. The clinking of the bar room glasses like nails on a chalkboard.

"Cabe!" The voice was Alana's. It came from his right. He forced himself to turn. The smile on his best friend's face was one of welcome and disbelief. "What are you doing here?"

"Surprise."

He moved on legs that felt as stiff as bar stool legs, nodding at Trent absently, his eyes settling on Saedra one more time. The song she'd been dancing to had just come to an end, and Saedra smiled at something Stewart "the jerk" had just said.

"Wow. That is a surprise. You hate places like this."

He pulled out a chair he didn't remember reaching for. "I know."

But Alana had followed his gaze, and she wasn't stupid. Neither was Trent because he did the same. They both turned back to him, a look of consternation on Alana's face.

"So that's the way the wind blows, huh?"

He shrugged. Why deny it? Honestly, he was glad the cat was out of the bag. Duplicity wasn't his forte. Never had been—never would be.

"What's Stewart doing here?" he asked.

Alana leaned close because Saedra was only a few feet away. "Saedra called him."

Ouch.

She hadn't seen him yet. He shook his head, wanting to confess everything to his best friend, knowing this wasn't the place or time. Later. He'd talk to Alana later. Maybe she could help him figure out what was going on because he sure as hell didn't get it. One minute Saedra was holding him tight, the next she'd flitted away with a man he'd thought she didn't like.

"Cabe!"

She'd spotted him. He stood up, held out a chair for her, ignoring Stewart. "Saedra."

He knew her well enough by now to spot the telltale signs of discomfort. A smile froze midway up her face. She glanced at Stewart quickly as if hoping he hadn't followed her from the dance floor. He had.

The man completely missed the tension in the air. "Our fearless leader," he said, coming forward and shaking Cabe's hand. "Come out to celebrate our success in bagging that buck, huh?"

"Uh, sure."

Saedra knew better, and she had the good grace to appear abashed. Not surprising given his words to her this morning. Clearly, this was her way of telling him to go take a flying leap.

"Can I get you something to drink?" Stewart asked.

The man stood out like a broken egg in his khaki-colored pants and polo shirt. All that was missing was the sweater tied around his neck. Every other male in the bar, including himself, had a cowboy hat on his head and boots on their feet. Not Stewart. Cabe glanced at the man's feet. Loafers. Big surprise.

"I'd love a glass of water." Saedra smiled at Stewart in gratitude. Cabe's stomach rolled.

Stewart headed to the bar after asking everyone what they wanted, too. Cabe almost ordered a shot of whiskey, straight up, but he'd never been much of a drinker.

The moment they were alone, Trent leaned forward. "Actually, I'm glad you're both here." Cabe caught the look Trent shared with Alana, their unspoken intimacy causing Cabe's insides to twinge, although for the life of him he didn't know why. "Alana and I have something we'd like to ask you."

His best friend leaned across the table, too. She glanced at her soon-to-be-husband, as if silently asking him a question and, when satisfied, turned back to them.

"We'd like for you to be our best woman and man of honor," she said.

Silence.

Cabe glanced at Saedra. She appeared as perplexed as he felt.

"Don't you mean best man and maid of honor?" he heard himself ask.

Alana smiled. "Nope. We're switching things up. Since you're my best friend, Cabe, and Alana is Trent's best friend, we thought it'd be fun if we did things a little different."

"Wow," Saedra said. "That's a cool idea."

Cabe wasn't so certain he'd call it cool. He liked things traditional, but Alana was his best friend and so whatever she wanted she'd get.

"Just don't ask me to wear a dress," he quipped.

Everyone laughed, all except Saedra; she appeared deep in thought. Behind her, Cabe saw Stewart turn away from the bar. A new song came on, a slow one.

Cabe stood abruptly. "Let's dance."

Saedra seemed to jerk in her seat. "What?"

He held out his hand. "Let's dance," he repeated.

"Cabe—"

"Go dance," Alana ordered. "We'll keep Stewart entertained."

Clearly, Saedra didn't want to go, but his friend pushed on her shoulder.

"Go. You're being rude."

Saedra went. She wasn't happy about it, Cabe could

tell, but she followed him to the dance floor nonetheless. When he turned and faced her, he wasted no time.

"You better have a damn good reason for ditching me tonight."

of her. He'd called and texted her, but nothing had
come of it. She remembered the days, when he'd called
her, then at her office and at home, but nothing.
He'd given up.

Chapter Thirteen

Panic.

It caused her heart to race crazily. Made her stomach do strange things. Stirred a desire within her to flee.

"I didn't ditch you." He pulled her up against him.

She almost gasped. There. It happened again. That
strange feeling, the one that reminded her of the time
she'd gone skydiving, when she'd been free-falling, the
earth drawing ever closer.

"Sure feels that way when you don't even bother to
call."

And tell him what? That he'd touched her heart last
night? That this morning his kiss goodbye had made
her toes curl? That what she felt for him scared the crap
out of her?

"By the way," he added, pulling her even closer, his
hips touching hers in an all-too-familiar way as an old
Garth Brooks song played, "I don't have your cell phone
number."

"No?" She felt him shake his head while she tried like
the devil not to feel utterly self-conscious as his thighs
brushed her own. "Well, Alana has it."

"Yeah. No kidding. How do you think I knew you
were here?"

She hadn't given it any thought. She'd been too stunned

to see him sitting at their table, the consummate cowboy with his ink-colored sideburns and his black hat. Too startled to come face-to-face with the man she'd been trying hard to forget all day. His final words to her this morning rang once again in her ears.

You're my woman.

She shivered.

"You cold?"

She drew back to look into his eyes. Despite telling her hands not to move, her fingers stroked the soft fabric of his button-down shirt, the color the same as his blue eyes.

"What are we doing?" She saw those blue eyes flare. "I mean, neither of us wants a relationship, right? So why do you care if I'm out with Stewart or not?"

"I *don't* care."

She snorted.

"You can do whatever you want."

"Then I guess you don't mind if I dance with Stewart again."

"Nope."

She stopped right in the middle of the dance floor. "You are such a liar."

He took a step back, but he didn't let her go. She saw him glance back at the table where Alana, Trent and Stewart sat, watching.

"I don't like sharing," he quickly amended.

"See, that's just it. You shouldn't mind what I do." She looked down at the floor, at a loss for words for a moment. "You're as much of an emotional wreck as I am."

Wait. That's not what she'd meant to say. Or maybe she had. Damn it. The man had her so confused.

"But why are *you* such a wreck?" he asked. "Hot one minute, cold the next."

"That's the pot calling the kettle black."

"Yeah, but I have a pretty damn good reason. What's yours?"

How could she explain it to him? How did one make a near-stranger understand all she'd been through? The lessons in life that had been taught to her by men weren't good. They couldn't be trusted. Even kindhearted and sweet men like Cabe. Heck, even her best friend, Trent. It'd taken a special woman like Alana to bring Trent around. She wished she was that kind of courageous, like Alana, but she'd been kicked in the teeth one too many times.

"I have my reasons, Trent. I wish you could trust me on that."

She broke out of his arms, sad and angry and miserable because she didn't want to feel this way. She didn't want to hurt him. That's why she'd made it clear right from the get-go what kind of woman she was. And then last night had happened and she'd held him and she'd found herself wishing things were different…that she was different.

"Saedra."

She kept walking, hoped nobody saw how close to tears she was, wondering why she gave a damn if someone did? There was a back door that she'd seen people go in and out of earlier. She headed for it now.

Cabe followed.

She sensed his presence, wished she'd driven to the bar in her own car so she could head to the front and simply drive away, but she was stuck.

"Saedra, stop."

Thank God she didn't actually cry because he stepped in front of her, and since there was a good-size moon overhead and lights in the parking lot, she could perfectly spot the consternation in his eyes.

"Sorry, sorry." She held up her hands. "I just needed a little air."

"What's wrong with you, Saedra? Why did you go out with Stewart tonight? You had to know that would bother me." He dragged a hand down his face. "I mean, shit, I know we're not talking marriage here, but after last night, the least you could do was wait until you left the ranch before going out with another man."

"Trust me, Cabe. It's better this way."

"So that's it, then? You're just going to ditch me for someone like Stewart?"

"I'll be busy. So will you. Before you know it, I'll be gone, and you'll thank me afterward, Cabe. You really will."

Beneath the starry sky she saw him shake his head, his eyes glancing heavenward for a moment before meeting her own again.

"Boy. Whoever he was, he sure did a number on you, didn't he?"

That was just it. It hadn't been a single man. It'd been a whole slew of bad choices.

"This was never going to be more than a one-night stand," she heard herself say.

He didn't say anything. Of course he didn't. What could he say?

"Are you in love with me, Cabe?" she asked, completely serious.

No answer.

"Of course not. You're still hung up on Kimberly. See? Disaster in the making. That's what this would be. I know it and you know it."

And this time when she turned back around, he didn't follow. This time, he didn't even call out her name. She wasn't surprised. What did surprise her, however, was the disappointment she felt.

HE DIDN'T GO back inside. What was the point? She was right. When she put things in perspective, it made a whole lot of sense.

Then why did he feel as if he'd made a mistake?

She was right. He didn't love her. He might never love someone again because, to be honest, he wasn't sure finding a love like he'd had with Kimberly could happen more than once in a lifetime.

But as he lay in bed that night, he felt something he hadn't felt in a long time…lonely. It didn't help matters that he heard Saedra come in an hour or two later. He'd been waiting up for her. Oh, he told himself it was to ensure everyone got home safe and sound, including his guest, but deep inside he knew that wasn't true. When he heard Trent's truck pull in, he listened for the sound of Stewart's vehicle, wondering if Saedra was inside. Before he thought better of it, he moved to the window, hanging back so he wouldn't be spotted, more relieved than he cared to admit when he spotted Saedra's golden head in the moonlight.

She hadn't gone home with Stewart.

A part of him had wished she had. It would have been easier to put everything behind him then. Easier to let her go if he'd known she'd been with another man. Instead, he heard her come inside, heard her feet on the stairs, waited, breath caught in his chest when she paused on the first landing, air gushing from his lungs when she moved on.

He wanted her.

His mind might warn him away, but his body had other ideas.

Sleep was a long time coming that evening. He spent

the entire night in a state of half sleep that left him tired and exhausted and out of sorts the next morning. Fortunately, all his guests had been grounded thanks to the weather report, which called for snow, but today was the all-important Christmas tree day, something he dreaded almost as much as he dreaded facing Saedra.

They were meeting early, which, after glancing out his bedroom window, was probably for the best, he thought. Given the look of the pewter-colored sky, they had three, maybe four hours—tops—before it started snowing. Once that started, it had a tendency to stick around for a bit.

"There you are!"

His daughter's excited blue eyes were the first things to greet him when he entered the kitchen a few minutes later. The delight those eyes contained was all the confirmation he needed that the day ahead was a big deal to her, just as Saedra had said.

"Where have you been?" She all but raced to the stove where she'd cooked up some scrambled eggs. She hurriedly scooped some onto a plate. "Alana and Trent were ready an hour ago."

"Sorry."

"Saedra's still sleeping, too. Did the two of you stay out too late last night?"

So she wasn't up, either. Interesting. Maybe she'd spent the night tossing and turning like he had.

Rana still waited for an answer, so Cabe said, "It wasn't 'the two of us' out, and I was home early. The other three were out late." Well, Stewart had been a part of that, too, but he didn't mention that.

Rana must have picked up on how out of sorts he felt because she frowned as she set the plate of eggs in front of him. He took a seat, telling himself he wasn't hungry, knowing he should probably eat. They had an hour's drive to where they usually selected a tree, then another hour or two of tromping through the hills, then more time to load the dang tree. What a fiasco.

"Is there something going on between the two of you?"

He glanced up sharply, eyes automatically narrowing. "What makes you say that?"

Rana shrugged. "You just seem, I don't know, irritated with her all the time."

He felt his brows lift. Was it that obvious? "There's nothing going on."

Liar.

He missed the days when Rana had been too young to understand adult undercurrents. These days she seemed entirely too mature for her own good.

"She's nice."

Of course she thought that. Saedra was Trent's best friend, and Rana adored Trent, so any friend of his was a friend of Rana's. Plus, she was a world-class barrel racer. His daughter lived and breathed rodeo. Add in the fact that she owned a cat—Rana had always wanted a cat— and you had the makings of some serious hero worship.

"She's not my type."

Rana's mouth dropped open. "Dad, if you're waiting for a *Sports Illustrated* cover model, it's not going to happen. Besides, Saedra's so beautiful she could *be* one of those models."

He glanced down at his eggs. The things tasted like sawdust, not because of Rana's cooking, but because he suddenly had no appetite.

"Nobody will *ever* replace your mom."

When he looked up, Saedra stood in the kitchen doorway, and for the briefest of moments he could have sworn he saw disappointment in her eyes, but he had to be mistaken.

"I would never even bother trying," he added, looking Saedra in the eye.

Chapter Fourteen

Of course he would never fall in love again, Saedra thought as they all piled into Cabe's truck. He'd told her as much last night, and that was fine. That was the way she wanted it.

Didn't she?

"I hope it snows," Rana said as she climbed into the back, her hair pulled back into a ponytail, a blue wool headband covering her ears, her jacket in the same color crinkling as she leaned forward in excitement. "There's nothing like going Christmas tree hunting in the snow."

Saedra had spent a sleepless night thinking about their conversation. Thinking about the hurt she'd seen in his eyes when she'd told him she wasn't his type. Thinking about the guilt she'd felt when she'd returned to Stewart, a man she didn't even like.

What is wrong *with you?*

"Let's hope it holds off for a little while," Cabe said, starting up the truck. "Bound to get cold."

He hadn't looked at her. Not once. Not after his comments in the kitchen. Rana had bounded up from her chair and served her some eggs when she'd spotted her standing there, but Saedra hadn't been hungry. By the time she'd taken a seat, Cabe had headed off to warm the truck up.

out a tree for the house. Besides, maybe Trent and Alana want to spend some time alone together picking out their own tree."

"No, no." Alana smiled from the backseat. "You two head out on your own. I want to spend time with Rana and my fiancé."

The three of them exchanged smiles, but when Trent caught her gaze, his grin started to fade.

"What is it?" he mouthed.

Saedra shook her head. She didn't want him to know what an utter fool she'd been. And how completely confused she felt this morning. After last night she should have been pleased that Cabe was doing as she asked— leaving her alone. But she wasn't happy. She was edgy and upset and stressed, and she knew it was all because of Cabe.

"I agree with Saedra." They were the first words Cabe had spoken in ages. "You should come with us, Rana."

"Daddy." The teenager peered up at him with what could only be called a cajoling smile. "You and Saedra should get to know each other better. You've spent hardly any time together."

Saedra almost laughed. If the teenager only knew.

"Rana—"

"Bye." She opened the truck's door and jumped out. In seconds she had the tailgate open and had pulled out a bow saw, holding it up like someone out of a Freddy Kruger movie. "Come on, guys," she said to Trent and Alana.

Alana and Trent exchanged an amused glance before Trent said, "I guess we've been given our orders," and opened the truck door. In moments it was just the two of them, Rana waving goodbye as they trekked to the left of the truck.

"Alrighty, then," Saedra heard herself mutter.

She glanced at Cabe, discouraged by the way his lips pressed together, how he glanced in her direction, only to shake his head. She understood. She really did. She'd rebuffed him last night. And before that she'd pulled that stupid move with Stewart. She didn't blame him for not wanting to hang out with her. Sometimes, she didn't want to hang out with herself.

It had started to snow. Not big flakes. They were tiny little dots that melted the moment they touched the windshield, and though she knew it was completely irrational, she wanted to wrench open her door, tip her head back and catch some on the end of her tongue. Man, she really had lost her mind.

"There used to be a good group of trees over that way." He pointed up the road a bit. "Let's try there first."

He hopped out, grabbed a second bow saw and turned toward their destination.

"You look like someone out of a horror movie," she quipped, deciding they needed to do something to lighten the mood. "You could do some serious dismembering with that thing, couldn't you?"

He didn't even glance back.

"I hear people frequently dump bodies in places like these." What a great Christmastime conversation, she thought. "I can see why."

His boots crunched on a blanket of dead pine needles in response. Her feet slid atop a patch of frost, and her cheeks stung from the cold. From her pocket she pulled out an off-white angora ski cap, tugging it on. That was better. She'd left her hair down specifically for their outdoor adventure. The long strands kept her neck warm.

"Hey, slow down."

He seemed to be on a mission, and she didn't blame him. Here he was with a woman he wasn't particularly happy with and doing something he'd more than likely dreaded since Alana had pronounced what they were doing.

"Cabe."

He finally slowed. She hurried to catch up, tiny dots of snow hitting her cheeks, some of them falling from the trees above her head.

"Look, I know you just want to get this over with, and I don't blame you, but if you're going to leave me in the dirt, I'd just as soon go back to the truck and wait for you there."

They were side by side now and she had a first glimpse of his face. Not happy. But he wasn't unhappy as in angry unhappy. No. He looked more stressed—like a person waiting in the lobby of a dental office.

"Or maybe you should go wait in the car. I'll pick out a tree and send Trent to cut it down."

He stopped sharply. "Why would I do that?"

She felt foolish then. Funny how you could be as intimate as possible with a person and still feel horribly uncomfortable in their presence.

"This must be hard for you." She peered up at him, and it was so difficult not to reach for his hand, to give it a squeeze, but it was better this way. Better to keep her distance...wasn't it?

"It's just a tree."

She knew he was about to bolt again so she stepped in front of him before he could move. "When was the last time you were here?"

She knew the answer. If she'd had any doubt, she could tell by the way his lips tipped down, but only for a moment, as if he'd wrestled with a sad smile, somehow managing to keep it from his face.

"Doesn't matter. Let's go."

"Cabe." Damn it. She caught his hand. It was cold. "We can go find the others if you want. Do this as a group if it'll make it easier."

"I'll be fine."

"You really loved her, didn't you?"

He tried to escape again. She wouldn't let him.

He looked heavenward, then at the ground, only to finally lock eyes. "She was my best friend."

She had no idea why the words hit her so hard, but they did, maybe because she'd recently lost her own best friend. Okay. She hadn't really lost Trent. The man was getting married. No big deal. At least the woman he'd picked was great. So she wasn't really losing him per se.

It felt like it, though.

It was her turn to look away. From somewhere deep inside, some deep cavern of her soul that she hadn't known existed, she admitted she was jealous.

Cabe is a really great guy.

He was. He was loyal. He was kind. He'd been the prefect husband by all accounts.

"She was a lucky woman," she heard herself say suddenly, and was unaccountably jealous of his dead wife. "I always seem to pick the wrong men."

She didn't mean him, she really didn't. She'd gone into her relationship with him with her eyes wide open. He'd done nothing wrong. Still, she sighed.

"Saedra," he said softly.

Why did she suddenly feel like crying? She had to turn away, but he must have seen something in her eyes because she heard him drop the saw.

"You make it sound like there's something wrong with you and there isn't." She heard him move closer. "Really, there isn't."

She nodded as if agreeing, but deep inside she had her doubts.

He tipped her chin up then and looked deep into her eyes as he said, "You're perfect."

His head began to lower. Inside, the words *no, no, no* rang out, but her heart had the opposite reaction.

Yes, yes, yes.

And she knew she kidded herself.

She liked this man. More than liked him, and it scared the cruddola out of her, so much so that she instantly drew back, but not away from him. No. Instead, she did something equally crazy. She rested her head on his chest. He took the hint, just held her. She closed her eyes, admitting she wanted to stand there all day, snow falling around them, forest so quiet you could hear a squirrel breathe, so quiet, in fact, that she could hear his heart beating beneath her ear.

A good heart. A kind heart. A loyal heart.

A heart a woman would be lucky to have.

Something like adrenaline buzzed through her. Something that told her she had a choice. She could step away and toward a future without him. Or she could take a chance. She could leap off a cliff, take a step toward love.

"They say once you've fallen for a person, you're twice as likely to fall in love again."

He didn't move.

"Really." Beneath her ear, she listened to the steady *lub-lub, lub-lub* of his heart. "I read an article about it. According to a well-known psychologist, a person has to have the right kind of brain. Something to do with dopamine and oxy-cotton-something-or-other. That's why some people fall in love and some people don't. Of course, the scientific study had nothing to say about why people fall in love with the *wrong* person. That's *my* problem, but as for you, there's no physiological reason why you shouldn't be able to get right back on the horse—so to speak."

Crazily, strangely, her words were making him relax. She could feel the tension slipping from his body.

"Saedra," he said.

"Yes," she whispered, her heart taking off like a windblown snowflake.

"Be quiet."

"I'm just saying."

"I know, but sometimes you talk too much."

"I do not."

She felt him shake, realized he was laughing, leaned back to admonish him some more.

Only he kissed her.

Chapter Fifteen

What are you doing?

That seemed to be the question of the week. One minute Cabe wanted nothing to do with her and the next all he wanted to do was kiss her, here, in a place that was special, a place he could never have imagined kissing another woman.

But kiss her he did.

She had the softest lips in the world, and the sweetest mouth he'd ever sipped, and a sultry tongue that drove him to distraction. He wanted to get close to her, to rest his hips in the apex of thighs, to maybe even press against her.

And still he kissed her.

He twined his tongue around her own. She moaned. He pulled back, took a breath, only to dive in and kiss her all over again, and Cabe knew this could get out of hand if he didn't stop now.

Somehow, he wrestled his lust to the ground, stepped on it, got it under control. He pulled back, took a deep breath, but couldn't seem to let her go. His hands. They were like glue. Stuck to her forearms. It confused and confounded and frustrated him so much it was all he could do to form a coherent thought.

"Damn," he muttered.

She seemed dazed, too, her eyes wide as she peered up at him, lips red from his kiss.

The snow fell harder.

"We better pick a tree before we get snowed in," he said.

The words brought to mind a warm fire, a thick rug and Saedra beneath him—probably not the smartest thing to think about right now. It was madness, this back-and-forth. The push and pull. The on-again, off-again. It wasn't right, either. They were better off forgetting about each other because no matter how many times he kissed her it was always there—the ghost of Christmas past. The ghost of Kimberly.

"You're right," he heard her say. "I would hate for us to come up empty-handed."

Was she talking about the tree? Or something else? He tried to find the answer in her eyes, failed, shook his head instead.

"Let's go."

He took yet another deep breath; that's what it took—another large gulp of oxygen—to give him the strength to step back from her. He bent down for the bow saw.

"There used to be a group of trees this way a few years ago. They were small. Bet they're a good size now."

That was better. Keep talking. Get your mind off how beautiful she looks in her little white ski cap, her pearlescent skin seeming to glow in the snowy half-light, the way her cheeks had warmed and turned as red as her lips. And behind her, around her, everywhere he looked… memories of Kimberly. There. The log where they'd all sat and had a picnic one year. Up ahead a little ways, a spot where his truck had gotten stuck. To his left the stump of a tree, the bottom sprouting new growth, a place where he'd cut a Christmas tree a few years back.

"Oh, Cabe, that one's beautiful."

For a moment he thought the words were a memory, but then he realized she had stopped. He followed her gaze and felt himself nod in agreement. Off the road a ways, surrounded by a group of smaller trees, was a perfectly shaped silver tip, its boughs crystallized by snow.

"Will it be too big?"

He shook his head. "No. It'll do."

When he looked down, she was smiling. His heart gave a lurch. He tried to tell himself it was because of her looks, but he knew better. The woman drove him nuts, but there was something about her that kept him coming back for more.

"You know, it occurs to me we're going to have to lug that thing back to the truck once you cut it down. How the heck do we do that?"

"Haven't you ever done this before?"

She pursed her lips. He felt himself smiling because she looked so young standing there all bundled up in her puffy jacket, snow sticking to loose strands of hair, cheeks red.

"Nope. Never."

"But you live in Colorado."

Her blond brows lifted. "What's that got to do with it?"

"You have lots of trees there."

She laughed. "That's like saying everyone owns a car in Los Angeles because everyone drives there."

He smiled, too. Amazing. A few seconds ago he wouldn't have thought it was possible, but suddenly he was thinking less about Kimberly and more about what it might be like to kiss Saedra again.

He glanced back at the tree. "I'll cut it down and drag it to the road. We'll bring the truck up here and load it in."

"Oh."

She was so dang cute when she wasn't driving him crazy. Not cute. Beautiful.

"Here we go," he said, hefting the saw.

It really wasn't as easy as it looked. He had to climb into tree branches at the base of the tree which, since it was snowing, was cold, wet work thanks to the snow that already clung to branches. He heard Saedra laugh when some of it got down his shirt, causing him to gasp. He was half tempted to gather some up and toss it in her direction, but they really did need to get a move on it. So he hacked and she drove him crazy—again—telling him where to saw. When the tree began to fall, she screeched and ran back. He knew the thing wasn't going to kill him and so merely stepped back a few feet, which made her cry out in warning.

"Relax," he said as the tree fell to the ground with a surprisingly gentle *whoosh*.

And it was done.

One ghost banished. New memories made. Christmas had returned.

He felt something touch his hand and glanced down. Saedra peered up at him.

"You'd make a hell of a lumberjack."

And he smiled. "Nah. I'll always be a cowboy."

"I know, but this could be a second career for you."

"What? Getting drenched by snow and smelling of pine needles? I don't think so."

"I'm just saying."

He wanted to hug her to him, not out of some caveman urge to kiss her, not even because he wanted to silence her, although there was that. No, he wanted to pull her up next to him because he was rapidly and crazily overwhelmed. *She'd* pushed him toward this moment. She'd been the one to wheedle and cajole and force him to face Christmas. Sure, the tree might have been Alana's idea, but it'd started with Saedra. She'd made this moment possible.

"Thank you," he said quietly.

"For what?"

He met her gaze, once again struck by her beauty. "For being you."

THANK YOU FOR BEING YOU.

Saedra hugged the words close to her as they rejoined their party, only half listening as Rana relayed the tale of how *she* was the one to find Alana and Trent's tree. Trent rolled his eyes and teased her about how she'd blindly picked whatever tree there'd been in the distance because she'd been worried about the snow. The three of them laughed, Saedra watching and thinking and wishing....

For what? That Cabe wanted more from her than sex. *You don't want that yourself.*

Still, as they all piled into the truck a short while later, she admitted to a twinge of jealousy. She was happy for Trent. She really was. If anyone deserved to find love, it was him. It was just bad luck that she seemed doomed to pick the wrong men.

"Saedra, you're quiet," Trent said from the backseat.

"They're both quiet," Alana added.

"Did you guys fight again?" Rana asked.

Fight? No. Kiss? Yes.

"I think we're both trying to defrost," Saedra said, glancing at Cabe in time to see him nod. "We were both freezing. We didn't have an energetic teenager to chase through the hills."

"Well, you picked a nice tree," Alana said. "Kimberly would approve."

Her stomach twisted. Another quick glance at Cabe revealed how his mouth had tightened. She was like the elephant in the room, this woman who'd stolen Cabe's heart.

"I can't wait to decorate it." She heard Rana wiggle in her seat. "It's been so long."

"Too long," she thought she heard Alana mutter.

The drive back seemed to take far less time than their drive out. The snow stopped, too, but she heard Alana say it would make its way to their little valley by nightfall. When they all hopped out of the truck she was surprised when Alana grabbed her arm.

"Come on," she said. "I know where the Christmas tree decorations are." She glanced toward Trent and Cabe and Rana. "They can handle the tree trimming and unloading."

This wasn't going to be easy on Cabe, she suddenly realized, the decorating and everything that went along with it. Too many memories. The tree had been bad enough, but now he'd be forced to unearth every personalized memento of his time with Kimberly. A special kind of torture, she admitted.

"What's the matter?" Alana asked.

Her eyes had started to burn. "Nothing," she said, inhaling sharply as the two of them drifted away, although Saedra could have sworn she felt Cabe's stare on her back. "I'm just an emotional wreck this week. It's the wedding. They always make me feel this way, and this one is the wedding of my best friend."

Alana seemed to buy the excuse. She clutched her arm tighter, leaned in close to her. "You're a good friend to Trent. You really are. I can't thank you enough for all you've done."

They were on the front porch, Alana opening the door, Saedra catching a glimpse of the Christmas lights that blinked and winked along the banister railing. It was still cloudy overhead, but enough light shone through the window to illuminate the interior of the house, and the special spot where they would put the tree—in front of the bow window.

"I just hope everything goes well," Saedra murmured, but she wasn't talking about the wedding. She meant what was coming. She knew it would be hard on Cabe. Knew he was already dreading it. She could tell by his body language on the way home.

"Are you kidding?" Alana said, heading toward the stairs. "It'll be great."

Didn't she know? Couldn't she tell her best friend was hurting? Apparently not. She wasn't surprised. Alana had her mind on other things. She could be forgiven for being a little self-absorbed, but only a little because in the next breath she said, "I'm glad Cabe didn't back out of getting a tree."

"I know." Saedra couldn't keep the concern out of her voice. "It was hard on him today. It's going to get harder still once we start decorating the tree."

"Hard on us all," she said.

"Rana seems to be taking it well."

"She's young. This type of thing…" Alana shrugged. "Kids seems to rebound faster. I've seen that a lot during my time as a therapist."

"Cabe seems determined to *never* get over it," Saedra muttered.

She hadn't meant to sound so disappointed, or disgruntled, but Alana paused outside Cabe's bedroom, and the memories of what she and Cabe had done in that room, combined with Alana's lifted eyebrows, caused Saedra to look anywhere but into Alana's eyes.

"What's going on?" Alana asked softly.

"Nothing." But she'd responded too quickly, taking

the next set of stairs two at a time. Alana followed, but Saedra still couldn't look the woman in the eye.

"Saedra." She pulled her to a stop outside her own bedroom door. Ramses must have heard them because he began to meow. "I might not know you as well as Trent, but I know disgruntlement when I hear it. Did you proposition Cabe?"

Saedra almost laughed as she remembered the way Cabe had pulled up in front of that motel. "I think it's safe to say *he* propositioned *me*."

Alana's mouth hung open a second. *"Cabe?"*

"Weeell, I encouraged him a bit." She glanced over the edge of the balustrade and down the stairwell. The men appeared to be outside still, but Saedra headed for her bedroom door just the same. Ramses couldn't have been more delighted when she opened the door, the cat winding himself between her legs, his trademark meow filling the room, and no doubt leaving a generous portion of his orange fur on her jean-clad legs. "You're going to need to sit down." She motioned toward the window.

"Is it that bad?"

"No." It felt good to have someone to talk to. Someone who knew Cabe. Someone who had carried her own set of baggage and who might be able to shed some light on Saedra's misguided life. She'd never had any girlfriends—just the friends she rode with.

"At first I just, you know, wanted to get under his skin." She took a seat at the window, Ramses instantly jumping into her lap. They were still down there—Cabe, Trent and Rana—examining the bottom of one of the trees that was still in the back of the truck and completely oblivious to the fact that they were being watched. Alana took a seat next to her, and Ramses, in typical Persian fashion, glanced over at Alana as if wondering who the peon was who'd dared to enter his domain. "But then I realized I was really attracted to him, so I sort of pushed the issue, but he was definitely the one to bring it to the next level."

"That level being...?"

The chill from the window made her blush all the more heated. "We went to a local motel." Alana's pretty light-blue eyes all but bulged. "I had no clue that he was going to do it."

"I'll be damned," Alana mused.

"It was supposed to be a one-time thing." Saedra shook her head. "But it wasn't."

"So you guys are dating?"

"No."

Alana appeared perplexed.

"I told him having me for a girlfriend was a bad idea."

And now she looked even *more* confused. "Why would you tell him that?"

From down below the sound of a chain saw filtered through the window. Ramses cocked his head. They all turned. Outside, Cabe sawed off a branch while Trent held the tree.

"It doesn't matter," Saedra heard herself say. "Even if I had been willing to take things further, Cabe made it clear he wasn't ready for more than a..." She swallowed against the ball of emotion that unexpectedly formed in her throat. "That he just wasn't ready for anything, but then he changed his mind, only I messed things up royally when I went out with Stewart, and then today things sort of changed and now I don't know what I want and I don't think he does, either."

"Because he's still hung up on Kimberly."

She shrugged, petting Ramses, who'd decided his back

legs were in desperate need of a cleaning. "So I backed off. Only…" She took a deep breath. "I just wish I…"

"That things were different?" Alana finished for her.

She gave a sharp shake of her head, pulling Ramses up to her chin and resting her cheek on him before he gave a mew of protest that his grooming session had been interrupted.

"That I wasn't so messed up," she admitted, setting the cat back down. "Maybe if I wasn't so screwy in the head, I could help him. Maybe I could steer him clear of the past. Maybe I could do for him what you did for Trent."

Alana's warm palm covered her own. Ramses sniffed her arm curiously. "Why can't you?"

"I think—" gosh, where had the tears come from? "—I'm too afraid." Was that shame staining her cheeks now? "It's been so long since I wanted to try."

"Try what?"

Why was her heart banging against her chest like wind chimes? "To love."

The fingers clutched her harder. "We're all capable of finding love."

"Yeah, but some of us are better at it than others." She shook her head.

"You could be good at it, too." She let her go. "With Cabe."

She'd stepped into the vacuum of space, that's how quiet everything went inside, so quiet that it felt for a moment as if time had stopped. "I don't think I'd survive getting my heart broken again."

"Cabe won't break your heart." Alana grabbed both her hands this time, much to Ramses's dismay, the cat protesting the sudden loss of contact by meowing once again. Saedra ignored him.

"I promise you, Saedra. There's not a better man out there. You just need to take a chance."

That was the problem, wasn't it? "I'm afraid."

"Don't be."

"And if it doesn't work out, then what?"

"You'll live through it."

Saedra laughed, petting Ramses again when Alana released her hand, the familiar motion doing little to soothe her, unfortunately. "Thanks. I feel buoyed with confidence now."

Alana leaned in close to her. "My point is, Saedra, what if you don't? What if you drive away after Trent and I get married? What if you look back and wonder...did I let a good man go? Will you be able to live with *that*?"

Deep down inside, Saedra already knew the answer, and it scared the crud out of her.

No, she couldn't live with that.

Chapter Sixteen

He'd never had a panic attack before, but he might be on the verge of one now.

"Here we go," Trent said, hefting the heavy end of the tree and turning toward the house.

"Can I help?" Rana asked.

They'd spent the past half hour getting the trees ready to go into the stand, and none too soon, too. The snow had finally arrived. Cabe glanced up at the sky and watched the flakes fall for a moment while Trent guided them up the steps of the porch and into the house.

He didn't want to go inside that house.

He knew what was coming and he knew it wasn't going to be much fun, a thought only reinforced when he stepped inside and spotted Saedra and Alana at the foot of the stairs, an assortment of familiar boxes at their feet, a pained look sliding onto Alana's face when she caught a glimpse of him. Was it that obvious what was going through his mind?

"We're setting it up in living room."

Not the family room. Not like what they used to do. He didn't know if that was good or bad. Honestly, he had a hard time identifying anything he felt right now. He'd gone numb.

"I think it'll be just as pretty in there," Rana said as

his gaze slid toward his daughter. She'd caught the undercurrents, too, or perhaps it had finally hit her that for the first time in nearly five years they were doing something uniquely tied to her mother.

"Let's get the boxes moved." Saedra punctuated the words with a wide smile. "Gentlemen, lead the way."

Trent caught his eye as he changed direction with the tree in hand, the man shaking his head in obvious amusement before heading toward the living room.

It helped, the change of locations. His stomach unclenched, his breaths came a little easier, his mood lightened. Not a lot, but a little.

Saedra placed the box down at the same time he helped Trent to stand up the tree. They'd judged the size just right, the top barely brushing the vaulted ceiling.

"I love it."

The words came from Rana, and she sounded so serious and yet so sad that Cabe immediately turned toward her. The tears in her eyes caused him to look away.

"Let's get started." Again, it was Saedra who spoke, her long blond hair nearly touching the floor as she bent and set the first box down, but she didn't immediately straighten. Instead, he saw her take a deep breath as she opened the lid.

He almost gasped.

They were instantly familiar. Instantly recognizable. There, on the top layer of a box made exclusively for ornaments, lay a silver star with a photo in the middle—Rana, Kimberly and him. There, too, was the glass ball that Kimberly had created the year she'd decided to take up ornament making, a disaster as evidenced by the way the colors she'd poured inside the ball all ran together in a soupy mess. She never did have patience. And there,

the tiny glass horse Kimberly had bought in San Fran-
cisco the first year they'd been married.

Dear God. If he'd thought the house decorations had
been hard to stomach, that was nothing compared to this.

"Oh, look, the horse. I've always loved that horse.
Uncle Brayden gave it to me, remember?" Rana came
forward and scooped the shiny souvenir from the box.
"When I was little, I used to hold it up to the light and
watch the rainbow prisms form on the ground." She did
that now, but it was too cloudy outside for it to work.
"Where are the lights?"

"Here," Alana said.

"We need to do that first, right, Daddy?"

He nodded absently.

"Here. I'll take one end. We can pass the strand back
and forth." Saedra held out her hands. "Where's the
plug?"

"Down there," Alana said.

Trent moved to stand next to him, clapped him on the
back, his voice low as he asked, "You okay?"

"Fine."

"How about a drink?"

"I don't drink."

"I think you might want to start."

That almost knocked a smile out of him. Almost. "I
think I'll let the ladies handle this."

He'd turned away before Trent said another word, and
he almost made it to the door before he heard Alana call
out, "Cabe, where are you going?"

"To get some air."

"I SHOULD GO after him," Saedra muttered for about the
tenth time since Cabe had left the room. "He didn't look
happy when he left."

They'd finished wrapping the lights, Alana and Rana and even Trent placing ornaments on the tree. Saedra glanced toward the door again, hoping Cabe would make an appearance, but the man was gone.

"He's hurting," Alana said, her voice pitched low so Rana didn't hear.

The teenager seemed oblivious to the fact that her father wasn't around. She was too busy oohing and ahhing over the various ornaments she pulled out of the box, in many cases explaining their significance, clearly delighted to get reacquainted with old friends.

"Maybe he needs someone to talk to."

Alana should go after him. She knew him the best, well, aside from Rana. That's what he needed right now: his best friend. But instead of running to console Cabe, she said, "So go," to Saedra.

"You think I should?"

"I think if I go after him we'll both end up crying." She held up a tiny Christmas angel. "This isn't easy for me, either."

No. Of course it wasn't. Trent must have heard her words because he came up to her, placed a hand on her shoulder. Alana glanced back and smiled.

"Where do you think he went?"

"My guess would be the barn," Alana said. "Or his office. That's where he goes to think most of the time."

She left without another word, as Rana exclaimed over yet another one of her cherished old friends. Kids really did handle grief differently than adults. Rana seemed content to celebrate every memory found in the box, while Cabe seemed determined to avoid them.

She checked his room before she left the house, grabbing her coat and giving Ramses a pat on the head before taking off outside. The snow had started to fall harder,

Saedra having to squint as she peered toward the barn, not that you could really see it from the house. Pine trees blocked the view. Thankfully her thick coat seemed to guard against the chill, and Saedra snuggled into it.

He wasn't in the barn.

She debated whether or not to beard the lion in his den, but her concern for him outweighed her objections, so up the stairs she went. She knew the moment she made it to the second-floor landing near the back corner of the barn that he was inside. She could see light shining from under the door, something that prompted her to let herself in without knocking.

"What the—"

She'd startled him, but he didn't seem angry that she'd followed him. No. The look on his face was more like indifference.

"Are you guys done?"

"No."

He sat in a chair before a window, a light on his desk illuminating his troubled face.

"I didn't think it'd be this hard."

She came forward. "I think it's been tough on us all in one way or another."

There were times when someone else's pain could cause a physical reaction. This was one of those moments, her insides crumbling in a way that nearly made her ill. The man had been through so much—and here she was picking at his wounds with a hot poker.

"I'll go away if you want me to."

He glanced up sharply. "No." He leaned forward, pretended to glance at a piece of paper on his desk. "I'm not very good company, though," he said as he flicked the paper away.

She came around his desk, her insides aching at the

sadness in his eyes. Should she hold him as she had earlier? They were alone now, she thought, glancing outside at the flakes that were falling and admitting that if she touched him her concern for him might turn into something more.

"Did you want to talk about it?" She sat on the corner of his desk.

"What's there to talk about? Once upon a time I was married. She died. End of story."

And that's all he wanted to say about that, she silently tacked on to the end of his sentence grimly, wondering if he'd ever get over his wife's death—and why it hurt so much to think he might not.

She glanced around the room, noting the utilitarian decor. Nothing fancy up here. Standard office furniture, Berber carpet, fluorescent lights overhead. The only ode to Western lifestyle was a saddle on a stand near the stairwell, the smell of leather filling the air.

"You used to rope competitively?"

He lifted his head as if surprised by the question. "A long time ago."

Too late, she remembered they'd been on their way home from a rodeo when "it" had happened.

To hell with it.

Maybe if everyone quit dancing around the subject, and stopped treating him with kid gloves, he'd start snapping out of it.

"You should come out on the road with me."

If she'd asked him to take off his clothes and dance the cancan he couldn't have given her a look more filled with condemnation, but you know what? It was better than his moping.

"I'm hardly in a position to leave the ranch, especially with my backup about to get married."

She crossed her arms in front of her. "You mean to tell me you can't hire someone to take over for you for a day or two?"

He let out a huff of condescending laughter. "This is my home. My blood, sweat and tears. I'm hardly going to turn it over to some stranger."

"Oh, and like no home-based business has ever closed up shop for a week so the owner could go on a cruise."

"This is different."

"It's not different. Hire someone to feed the livestock for you, don't book any guests for a few days and start competing again."

His eyes grew dark. "I'm not interested in rodeo anymore."

It took her a moment to realize why the words filled her with such dismay. She'd been half hoping he'd want to come watch her ride. After all, she'd just sold damn near everything she had so she could make a bid for the National Finals Rodeo next year. Sure her new horse might be back home in Colorado, and she might be giving him the winter off, but that didn't mean she wouldn't hit it hard one day soon.

So what do you care if he's not interested?

She *did* care.

Rodeo was such a huge part of her life. She'd never had the courage to do it full-time—until Dustin had died. Watching Trent battle back from death, realizing that life was too short, remembering how many times Dustin had encouraged her to live her dreams. Going to the NFR was her dream, and if Cabe didn't want any part of that, so be it. Forewarned was forearmed.

"I should get going." She stood. "I promised Rana I'd make her pulled pork for dinner and that needs to cook for a while."

He didn't follow. She didn't expect him to, but when she paused at the top of the stairwell, she found herself turning back to him.

"Sooner or later, Cabe, you need to get over her."

He jerked his head up.

"This dwelling in the past isn't healthy."

His eyes narrowed before he said, "This from the woman who can't commit to anything more than a one-night stand."

She nodded. "I know. You're right."

His brows lifted.

She forced herself to smile. "Alana and I talked and she helped me to realize I need to move on, too. But that's the difference between you and me. I'm willing to give it a try and you're not. I'm living, Cabe. I haven't holed myself up on a ranch in the middle of nowhere refusing to go anywhere and do anything unless I'm forced to do so. I'm living." She straightened to her full height. "You should, too."

Chapter Seventeen

His guests were leaving this morning, and Cabe couldn't have been more grateful for the distraction. After yet another sleepless night he'd woken up exhausted and out of sorts, Saedra's words ringing in his ears. She was wrong, of course. He'd moved on. He'd expanded the ranch, started a new business and these days he devoted his life to raising his daughter.

He had a good life.

Then why did he wake up feeling so empty? The feeling only worsened when he spotted the Christmas tree in the living room. He'd avoided it when he'd left to tell his guests goodbye an hour earlier. Now he stood at the entrance to the room, spotting the familiar relics of his past, his feet moving despite his best efforts to keep them planted on the ground. The closer he got, the more it smelled like Christmas, and the harder it was to keep moving.

"It looks good, doesn't it, Daddy?"

He drew himself up. "It does."

Rana came forward, stopping beside him. "I think Mom would be happy Christmas is back again."

Yes. She probably would. And angry with him that he'd kept it out of their daughter's life for so many years.

"The tent's supposed to arrive today." Rana smiled up

at him, and he could tell she strove to change the subject, and to turn his mind from the past. "Alana said I can go with her and Trent to fetch Trent's mom from the airport, if her flight isn't canceled. I guess we got a lot of snow."

"We're still getting snow."

He'd been out in it when he'd waved his guests goodbye, including that damn Stewart, thank God, but it shouldn't be enough to dampen wedding plans.

"I was thinking, Daddy, that we could maybe go on our Christmas ride, you know, like we used to do."

The Christmas ride. Lord help him. He hadn't thought of that in years.

"I guess things are going to get pretty crazy around here what with all the guests arriving and things to do for the wedding. Not to mention Alana hasn't found a dress so we still need to search for one of those, and Christmas Day is the wedding, so we won't be able to ride then. Today's really our last day to go. Do you mind?"

He wanted to say no. There were so many things to do, but the look of eagerness on Rana's face was his undoing.

"I guess we could."

The smile she gave him was his reward. "I'll go tell everyone." She shot off.

"Wait, wait, wait," he called. "I thought it'd be just you and me?"

"Just us? Nah. That wouldn't be any fun. We all need to go."

"But what about Trent's mom?"

"She won't be coming in until later this afternoon. We have all morning to ride."

He could have thought of a million excuses, could have told her he had guests to supervise and cabins to make sure were clean and supplies to buy before their wedding guests started to arrive, but wouldn't that be doing exactly what Saedra had accused him of doing? Not living? Not embracing life? Work, work, work—that's all he ever did; that's what she'd been implying.

"A short ride," he heard himself say. "That's all."

"Hooray!"

She spun away again. He heard her head to the back door and Alana's house, no doubt to tell her the good news, Cabe following her out of the room.

Saedra was at the top of the stairs.

"That was nice of you."

You need to live.

He was trying. Lord help him, this past week he'd been trying harder than ever before, all thanks to Saedra.

"You're coming, right?"

She looked like she might decline, and Cabe tensed as she headed down the stairs. "You sure you want me to?"

"I think Rana would be disappointed if you didn't go."

"But not you?"

What was she asking? She'd made it clear they would never be anything more than friends. So what did she care if he wanted her to go along or not?

"We should all go," he said by way of a nonanswer.

It wasn't the response she'd been looking for, but damn it, he didn't know what else to say.

"Then I guess I'll go."

"Good."

They had a two-hour window to ride, although to be honest, Trent's mom might not need to be picked up at the airport if it didn't stop snowing soon, Cabe thought, glancing up the barn aisle while he saddled his spotted gray horse inside his stall. Alana did the same in the stall next to him. Trent was already up on his favorite horse, Baylor.

"Maybe we should wait," he told everyone. "It's coming down harder than yesterday."

"It'll be fine," Rana said as she finished brushing her horse in the stall across from his own. "I just hope everyone dressed warm."

His daughter had taken her own advice, Cabe noticed. She wore a silk "ragweed" scarf that was wrapped around her neck, one that was maroon and matched the thick Carhartt jacket she'd donned, her black hat spotted by snow. He'd dashed snow off his own beige Resistol before coming in the barn.

"It gets cold quick out there," she told Saedra, who'd walked into the barn bundled in her own fluffy jacket.

"I think I'm wearing enough layers to fill a thrift store," Saedra said. "Unfortunately, I didn't bring a cowboy hat so my ski cap will have to do."

She looked lovely, he thought as she stopped outside his stall. The cold had turned her cheeks red, her blue eyes more pronounced with her hair pulled back from her face.

"What horse do you want me to ride?"

"I saddled up Marigold for you. She's in the stall next to Alana's horse." He paused a moment to tighten the girth of his own animal. Ghost didn't like it too tight, the gelding pinning his ears, a back leg kicking out and sending pine shavings through the air. Cabe ignored him. "I don't know if she's ever been ridden in the snow, though. Might be a handful."

"That's okay." She cocked a brow at him. "I'm not afraid of a challenge."

He was right in the middle of grabbing Ghost's bridle, but he froze, wondering at the look on her face. If he didn't know better, he'd have sworn she'd just thrown down a gauntlet of some sort.

She disappeared from view, Cabe staring after her for a moment.

Five minutes later they were all mounted up, Trent saying, "It's about time," as Cabe led his horse from the barn. "I'm freezing out here."

"Hey, you're the one that saddled up too quickly," Rana teased. "Serves you right if you're cold."

Trent patted his horse, though he wore thick gloves and looked every bit as bundled up as Rana. "I know, I know."

They all mounted up, Rana announcing they were going to ride the road toward the cabins, then follow the fence line around and back to the barn. It was an easy ride, and the road would be easy to follow even with snow accumulating on the ground. Plus, they would be back in less than an hour.

"Let's go," Rana said with a huge grin, spurring her horse into a lope. Trent and Alana followed suit, but Cabe held back. So did Saedra, looking down at her horse and patting its red neck.

"She seems fine in the snow," Saedra said.

"Good."

"How long have you had her?"

"A couple weeks."

"Come on, you guys, catch up," Rana yelled from the end of the driveway, snow making her look blurry in the distance.

Cabe nudged his horse into a jog. Rana disappeared around the corner and down the main road.

"She's having a ball," Saedra observed.

"This isn't as tough for her as it is for me."

Where had those words come from?

Saedra pulled her horse up for a second, reaching across and patting him on the thigh. "It'll get easier, Cabe."

He nodded. "So I hear."

They trotted along in silence.

"It'll only get easier if you let it," she said.

They were at the end of the drive that led to the barn, and when they rounded the corner, he could see through a flurry of flakes that the other three had slowed down. Alana's laughter filled the air. He saw Trent reach out for her, the two of them clasping hands for a moment. Cabe glanced over at Saedra, noting that she'd spotted the gesture, too.

"Three more days," she said, "and then the two of them will be official. Can you believe it's almost here?"

He was ready for it all to be over.

"I can't wait for you to meet Trent's mother. You'll love her."

Four more days. Everyone would be gone then. He'd get his life back. Saedra would be gone, too.

"I just hope the snow doesn't get any worse. We have so many people driving in from out of state."

Slick roads. Locked-up brakes. Car sliding off the road.

He tried to shut the memories out.

"Cabe, what's wrong?"

The reins suddenly dug into his hand.

"What'd I say?"

"Nothing."

But he answered too quickly. Too harshly. He kicked his horse into a lope.

"Cabe, stop."

She shouldn't have been able to catch up, not riding a strange horse, but he should have known better. She wasn't a champion barrel racer for nothing, and the sorrel horse was more handy than he could have ever known, the little mare leaping ahead of him and blocking his path, much to his own horse's surprise. His gelding left twin tracks in the snow he stopped so hard.

"What is it?" she asked again.

"It's not like I want to remember."

She straightened suddenly in her saddle. "Kimberly and Braden."

He didn't need to say anything. She'd figured it out on her own. "Cabe. I'm so sorry. Damn it. I'm always saying the wrong thing."

He took a deep breath. Snow fell, looking like mist in the distance, obscuring his view of Rana and the others.

"You were right."

She shot him a puzzled stare.

"Last night." He shook his head again. "I need to let it go." He rested his hand on the saddle horn. "I need to get over the deaths of my wife and brother. I need to let them go. I need to let *Kimberly* go."

He thought he heard her gasp.

"I've just been holding on to her for so long, I don't know how to do that." A snowflake landed on his arm. He absently brushed it away. "But I think it's time to try."

She smiled.

He squeezed his horse forward. She fell in alongside of him, but they rode in the snow for a good five minutes before he heard her say, "I'm glad."

IT WAS A RIDE Saedra knew she would never forget. Nothing beat riding in the snow. There was a stillness about it, the falling flakes seeming to shield them from sound; only the gentle crunching of their horses' hooves as they compressed the snow filled the air. Alana, Trent and Rana seemed content to stay ahead of them, no doubt intentionally, Alana glancing back at them from time to time.

"How long have you known Trent?" Cabe asked.

Her horse snorted. Saedra patted the mare's neck. "All my life."

He hadn't known that. She could tell by the surprised eyes beneath the brim of his hat.

"I grew up in what I affectionately like to call Trailerville, just outside of Denver, one of those places where they rent an itty-bitty space to anybody with a Winnebago."

"How'd you meet Trent?"

They'd made it to the river, the cabins Cabe rented out to people on their left, no lights on inside. Rana had told her all their guests had left, which meant plenty of space for wedding guests if need be.

"He lived next door."

"Trent grew up in a trailer?"

She smiled. "Nope. He lived about forty miles away, down the road, but we were so far in the middle of nowhere he was the closest thing to a neighbor we had. And his family had horses. I was born horse crazy. My mom never understood where I got it from. Maybe my father. He didn't hang around long enough for me to find out."

"That's where you learned how to ride? From Trent?"

They'd started jogging their horses again, Saedra looking ahead and realizing the other three had once again started loping. If they weren't careful they'd lose sight of them. Or maybe that was the plan.

"Actually, I learned how to ride from Trent's mom. She sort of adopted me. I'd disappear for hours over at their place, not that my own mom cared, so Trent's mom took me under her wing. She's an amazing lady. I don't know what I would have done without her. Suffice it to say my own home life wasn't all that great."

"What about Trent's dad? What happened to him?"

"Died when he was young. Tractor accident. Trent doesn't talk about it much. Neither does Gretchen."

"I take it she never remarried?"

She peeked over at him. "No, but she has a boyfriend. He lives in Denver. She says they're too old and set in their ways to marry, but I guess they've talked about it."

He didn't say anything, and Saedra wondered if he was thinking about Kimberly, once again jealous of the woman. *She* wanted Cabe. Only she feared she might never have him. He'd vowed to move on, but she wasn't convinced he'd be successful, which left her where, exactly?

A day late and a dollar short.

"Anyway," she said, trying to ignore the sudden pounding of her heart. "When my mom remarried and moved to Denver I still visited the ranch. I spent my summers helping out, learning to ride there, and how to run a ranch. Bought my first horse when I was fourteen with money I earned working for Gretchen."

They were farther down the road than she'd ever been before, the pine trees closing in on them, an occasional flurry of snow dropping from their branches. It grew colder all of a sudden. She shivered.

"You okay?"

"Just cold." And worried. Always worried about the future. She was taking an awful chance with him, and given her track record, she wasn't terribly optimistic it would all work out.

"You want to turn back?"

"No, no."

So they rode on, Cabe seeming to be content to keep quiet, and that was okay with Saedra. Eventually they caught up with the main group, though only because they'd had to stop and open a gate.

"Come on, you guys, keep up," Rana said, trotting off the moment they had the gate closed.

Honestly, moving felt good, so this time she followed Rana's lead. They kept sight of a trail that ran along the fence line, one remarkably free of snow thanks to the deer and other wildlife that must keep it groomed. They were climbing, but not a lot. The snow seemed to lighten up, so much so that she could see the ranch in the distance to her left, and from this angle another house to the northeast, a plume of smoke rising from its chimney, everything—as far as the eye could see—covered in white.

She was so enchanted by the view she didn't even realize they'd stopped until Cabe said, "Not a bad place to shut yourself off from the world, huh?"

She glanced over at him, a backdrop of white mountains causing his form to stand out, his breath misting in the cold.

"Not bad at all," she said.

"I don't know about you guys," Alana said, "but I'm getting cold. I say we cut through the pasture instead of following the fence line around."

They moved off as a group, the snow at least a foot deep off the beaten path, the horses having to work to get their footing, but it was wonderful. Her cheeks might be frozen. Her hands felt ready to fall off, but when they passed through yet another gate, this one not far from the back of the barn, she was disappointed it was all over.

"I think we all need hot cocoa," Rana said.

"Hear, hear," Alana said.

"I'm going to ride ahead and start the microwave in Dad's office."

She didn't even wait for a response. That was okay with the adults, although Cabe held back from the group when they started to follow in her wake. Saedra met his gaze curiously.

"I know another way we can warm up," he said. The

heat in his eyes warmed her to the core. "You could meet me at one of the empty cabins."

She could, but suddenly her feet were cold for an entirely different reason. "When?"

"After I untack my horse I'll tell everyone I'm going down to check on a guest. Meet me at cabin seven."

This was it, then, the moment when she decided, truly decided, to either go for it or not, because she kidded herself if she thought she could sleep with Cabe again and not fall even deeper.

That was why her heartbeat skittered off all over again when she took a deep breath and heard herself say, "Okay."

Chapter Eighteen

Move on.

The words kept playing over and over in Cabe's head as he made his way toward cabin seven. Still, he couldn't help feel like a teenager sneaking off with a girl when he let himself inside.

He immediately turned on the heat. The previous guest had left yesterday, but this cabin was one of three that had a fireplace. He set to work making a small blaze in the hearth, a part of him wondering if Saedra would show up, yet another part of him worried she would.

Worried, why?

He sat back on his heels, watching as a tiny flame turned into a bigger one thanks to some dry timber. Worried because he didn't know where this would lead. Worried because he didn't want to hurt her. Worried because there were no guarantees that he'd be able to move on.

"You in there?"

He'd left the door unlocked, but she must have figured otherwise because she still stood outside. Cabe straightened away from the fire and faced the door.

Now or never.

Deep breath. One step. Two steps. Open door.

"Hi," she said, blue eyes wide.

She sounded breathless, as if she'd run down from the

barn, and maybe she had. She hadn't changed, still wore her knit hat and her fluffy jacket. Still looked every bit as beautiful as she had on horseback. Still made him feel things he hadn't felt in a long while.

"Can I come in?" she asked, those eyes filling with humor.

He felt his cheeks blaze. He'd been so busy staring, he'd forgotten to step aside, something he did immediately. Only once she was in, he felt as self-conscious as a fifteen-year-old.

"Fire feels nice." She shrugged out of her jacket and pulled off her hat, tossing both onto a chair before holding her hands out to the flames.

"Do you want a drink?"

She turned to look at him, and was that amusement he saw in her gaze? Amusement and perhaps tenderness.

"No."

He could use one. Nerves. That's what he had—a severe case of the nerves. But why? He'd made love to her before. Shoot, she'd held him in her arms when he'd broken down. Of course, she'd bolted from his arms and straight into Stewart's, but she'd been scared. He was scared, too.

"You sure I can't get you something?" He pointed toward the kitchen. "Pretty sure there's some hot cocoa in there."

"Cabe."

His hand dropped to his side.

"Quit talking."

It was one of the things he loved about her, the way she dove right into things. Just like she would dive into qualifying for the National Finals Rodeo—but he didn't want to think about that, so when she stepped up to him and lay a hand against his cheek the way she'd done so many times in the past, he didn't move away. He wouldn't do anything to spoil this afternoon. Her other hand reached behind his head, drawing him down, and even though he told himself to take it slow, his hands instantly moved to her sweater, tugging it over her head, disappointed to realize she had a shirt on underneath.

"Here." She pulled the second shirt up and over. He started unbuttoning his shirt. She slipped off her boots next. He did the same, and suddenly it wasn't slow at all. Suddenly he couldn't get his clothes off fast enough and neither could she. When they came together again it was a shock to feel her bare body against his own, well, bare but for her underclothes and his own Jockey shorts.

"Bedroom," she said.

Yes, bedroom. The sooner, the better, because in his present frame of mind he might just push her up against a wall as he'd done the first time he'd kissed her.

The memory of that first kiss had him tugging her toward the room. She didn't head for the bed, though, much to his surprise. No, she went into the bathroom, pulled open the glass door and turned on the water.

He almost laughed. Leave it to Saedra to do something unexpected.

"What?" she asked.

"You're not shy."

She smiled. "Never have been. Never will be."

He liked that. She wasn't afraid to take charge, something that was so completely opposite of Kim—

No. He wouldn't think of her. Not now.

It was easy to think of something else, especially when Saedra reached behind her. He knew what was coming next, felt his own need begin to build as she slowly released the straps of her bra, her breasts spilling free.

"You're so beautiful," he heard himself groan.

"You're just saying that because you're about to get lucky."

And there he went almost laughing again. "True." And yet not true because there was far more to her beauty than the physical.

Steam began to billow from over the top of the door. She turned, slipped her underwear off, adjusted the water, then slid inside. He watched as water began to slide down her body, her long blond hair turning dark beneath the spray, rivulets forming and running between her breasts.

Damn.

He couldn't wait any longer. He hardly remembered taking off his underwear. The water made him gasp, its heat seeming more pronounced thanks to his chilled body, but she felt even hotter when he pulled her up against him, her blue eyes wide and full of amusement again.

"Slow down there, cowboy, I have plans for you."

She forced him to turn around, something warm and slick sliding up his back.

Her tongue.

He about gasped. "Jeez, woman."

One of her hands slid around the front of him, and Cabe waited for her to touch him, hardly able to breathe as she did so, but she didn't touch him there. No. Her fingers grazed his abdomen, skirted the band of muscles along his belly, slid up and up, something that smelled faintly of honey filling the shower.

Soap.

It wasn't her fingers touching him, it was a bar of soap, the slick feel of it surprisingly erotic, especially when she reached around him and used her other hand to spread it all over his body.

When would she touch him?

He ached for that touch, waited breathlessly as her free hand slid down, and then farther down until at last…bliss.

"Saedra," he groaned.

Her fingers worked magic. Cabe had to brace himself against the front of the shower to keep from falling down. She bent with him, one hand continuing its soapy assault, the other running up the length of him, then down, then up again.

He wouldn't last.

Water sluiced over him. He hardly noticed. All he felt were her fingers around him, the heat of her flesh and the warmth of her breath. He tried to turn around. She wouldn't let him.

"Don't move," she warned.

He wanted push her up against the shower wall, to lift her up so she would wrap her legs around him, to slide her down his length, but she kept him there, stroking him, softly at first, then harder and harder.

"Let it go, Cabe."

He didn't want to, but he was helpless beneath her touch. Her grip tightened, then released. His hips jerked. Up. Down. Tighten. Release. He moaned. She couldn't, wouldn't, release him and he knew, he just knew—

"Saedra."

His release came so hard and so fast he damn near wilted. Her body helped to prop him up as he throbbed and throbbed and throbbed.

"Good boy," she murmured.

Good boy?

"Now I think it's my turn."

He straightened and turned around before she could stop him, Cabe pushing her up against the shower wall so quickly she gasped.

"Oh, it's your turn all right."

She glanced up at him, blue eyes wide, hair drenched, and he'd never seen anything more beautiful in his life. He entered her. Hard.

He wasn't going to take it slow. He refused to be easy on her. He pressed her up against the wall at the same time he withdrew, only to thrust into her again.

"Yes, Cabe," she cried out again.

Her legs wrapped around him. He held her, dove deep, withdrew, deep again, and her cries grew louder and louder and Cabe knew he was going to explode again.

"Now," she moaned.

Yes, now. Together. The two of them. They crested the precipice, jumped off together, fell back to earth as one, and nothing had ever felt so sweet in Cabe's life.

Nothing.

SHE DIDN'T WANT to leave his arms.

Somehow, she didn't know how, exactly, they ended up in the cabin's bed, making love one more time before she'd collapsed against him, their heartbeats slowly returning to normal.

"You're going to be the death of me," he murmured, his voice rumbling beneath her ear. "A good death, though," he added.

She smiled. Yes. She wouldn't mind dying this way, either.

"I could stay here all day." She nuzzled his chest.

"Me, too."

"Dad?" A knock followed the word. "You in there?"

Saedra shot up. For some reason she jerked the covers up even though she knew Cabe had locked the front door.

"Hang on," Cabe called out. He burst from the bed

so fast he darn near took the covers with him. "Where are my pants?"

"In the family room."

"Shit."

"Why are you whispering?"

He shot into the family room, returning with an armful of clothes, some of which he tossed in her direction. "I don't want Rana to hear you."

She jerked back in surprise. "Why not?"

"Not now," he said.

Not now, what? she wanted to say, but he seemed so genuinely panicked she didn't think it was the time to argue the point.

She would have to give him credit; he dressed in record time, looking back and saying, "Stay," as he closed the door behind him.

"What?" she muttered. "Am I a dog now?"

She heard him answer the door. Heard Rana's voice ask what he'd been doing. He gave her some excuse about working on a leaky showerhead, and since his hair was still a bit damp, she would bet Rana bought it. Saedra heard something about the tent arriving, as she slipped from the covers, half tempted to simply get dressed and open the bedroom door with a jovial, "Surprise!" but she knew Cabe would kill her if she did that.

A minute later the front door closed, Cabe returning to the bedroom in time to see her slip on her sweater. To be honest, she'd become a little steamed by then, and she had to work to keep her voice even as she asked, "What did she want?"

Cabe appeared relieved. "The truck driver called. Apparently the wedding tent will arrive in about a half hour. She was looking for you."

"What'd you tell her?"

"That I hadn't seen you."

"Cabe!"

"What?" Light from the bedroom window revealed the confusion in his blue eyes.

She shook her head. "What are we doing here?"

He went into classic defense mode, arms crossed, face closed. "What do you mean?"

"This," she said, motioning to the bedroom. "What is this? What are we doing?"

His confusion faded. "We're getting to know each other."

"You said last night you were ready for more. Is that still true?"

"I am ready. I just don't want to rush into anything."

She told herself to calm down, forced herself to take a deep breath. "So what does that mean? More sneaking off in the middle of the night? 'Cause I have to tell you, Alana knows."

"She does?" His eyes went wide.

"It's because of her that I'm here, with you, scared to death that you're never going to be able to move on, but willing to give it a try."

His whole face softened, his eyes sweeping over her face, his mouth lifting a little around the edges. "And I'm glad."

Then why won't you let Rana know about us?

Patience, she told herself. Time would be her friend. She knew that, tried to reassure herself that she wasn't making a mistake, but it was so damn hard to have faith in herself...and him.

"So what's the game plan, then?" she asked. "Do we continue sneaking around? And what about after the wedding? What then?"

He closed the distance between them, pulling her into his arms. "One day at a time." He drew back. "That's what I need to do. Take it one day at a time."

It was only as he left her there in the cabin, alone, that she began to wonder if one day at a time would be enough.

Chapter Nineteen

He treated her like a near-stranger the rest of the day. Okay, that wasn't exactly true. He gave her a private smile when she arrived at the house, and Rana demanded to know where she'd been. Saedra blushed and said, "I was using the phone in Cabe's office."

Lies, lies, lies...but Rana clearly believed her because she said, "Oh. I didn't even think about checking there."

Cabe had suspected as much, which is how they'd come up with the excuse. Still, it irked her to no end to have to lie.

Alana didn't buy it, though. When a big moving-type truck pulled up to the barn less than an hour later, Cabe and Trent acted as guides as a clearly inexperienced driver backed the truck up the driveway.

"So," Alana asked over the *beep-beep-beep* of the backup lights. "Where'd you disappear to earlier?"

They stood outside the barn with Rana, all bundled up in their outdoor gear once again and watching as Cabe and Trent walked alongside the truck.

"I was in Cabe's office, following up on some last-minute details."

Alana glanced at Rana before shooting her a look that said, *Yeah, right.*

Saedra tried not to blush, but it was impossible. The

woman knew exactly what she'd been up to with Cabe, although she clearly picked up on the fact that Saedra and Cabe didn't want Rana to know.

"I'm just trying to button down a few more details before all our guests start arriving," Saedra said, trying to change the subject.

It worked.

"I know. It's going to be crazy, and I still haven't found a dress."

"I told you, wear my mom's dress."

The two of them glanced at Rana. This was the first time Seadra had heard mention of Kimberly's wedding dress, and Rana's permission to wear it, but the thought of that happening didn't sit well with Saedra. Not at all.

"Have you talked to your dad about that yet?" Alana asked. "Like I asked you to do?"

"Well, no." Rana snuggled deeper into her jacket, her brown hair spilling out over the collar of her jacket. "I was thinking it could be a surprise."

Oh, dear God, no.

"I'm pretty sure Cabe would want to weigh in on the decision," Saedra advised. "I'm sure your mother's dress is special to him."

"Yeah," Alana echoed. "Saedra's right."

Rana frowned. "It's really my dress. My dad gave it to me, but I'll ask him if you want. Dad!"

"Not now," Saedra instantly protested. "He's busy."

Cabe glanced over at them, but the truck had stopped backing up, the driver slipping out. Actually, there were three people in the cab of the truck, one of them sliding up the rear roll-up door while Cabe walked toward him.

Crap. She didn't want to be around for this discussion. She'd had her fill of seeing Cabe in pain.

"I told Alana she could wear Mom's wedding dress."

She wasn't wrong. His eyes revealed his every thought, some of which was surprise coupled with dismay. "We still have it?"

"It's in the attic," Rana said.

The attic. The location of so many forgotten memories. "Will it fit?"

"Cabe," Alana said, her voice soft. "There's really no need. I was thinking I might wear a denim skirt and cowboy boots. Goodness knows, that's about as dressy as I get."

"It's Rana's dress," he said. "She can do what she wants with it."

"Hooray!"

Yet, Rana's joy brought him no pleasure. He hadn't wanted to agree. She could tell by the way his eyes skated over the ground, never once looking any of them straight in the eye.

Clearly Alana had spotted the same thing because she said, "I'll think about it."

Cabe didn't say anything as he returned to supervising, but Saedra thought he seemed glad to get away, and he kept his distance the rest of the time they unloaded, too.

"You think he's upset about the wedding dress?"

"No." It was a lie, but she didn't want Alana feeling bad. "I think he's just stressed out about the wedding."

That was certainly true, although if she were honest with herself, she worried there was more to it than that. He might act as if he wanted to move on, but the whole thing with Rana didn't sit well.

"Hey," Trent said, shooting her a smile before grabbing his future wife's hand. "My mom's plane is on time."

"Seriously?" Alana asked. "That's great. I thought for sure this snow would cause a delay."

Trent glanced at his watch. "We gotta leave if we're going to get to the airport in time." Trent caught Saedra's eye again. "You want to come?"

"No, no." She waved her hands. "You two go ahead. Cabe and I can help these guys set up the tent."

There was really nothing for them to do, Saedra realized later. All they had to do was tell the guys they wanted the structure set up in the middle of the snow-covered arena. The rental company had assured them it would all work out beautifully, especially with the portable parquet floor they unloaded next and some portable heaters. She sure hoped so.

Two hours later the workers already had the frame assembled. No more snow fell and by the time they were done, the snow beneath the tent was already tromped down and beginning to melt.

"Oh, my!" Saedra's spirits suddenly lifted because she recognized that voice. "This is lovely."

Gretchen Anderson. Trent's mother.

"This will be perfect for the wedding," Gretchen said.

When the older woman turned, Saedra's eyes met hers, eyes the same as Trent's.

"Saedra!" she said, coming forward, hands outstretched. "I should have known you'd come up with something great."

She wanted to cry.

The woman who had taken the place of her own mother was all smiles and all Saedra wanted to do was sink into her arms. Gretchen knew her like no other person on earth, well, save Trent. Only she couldn't speak to Trent about Cabe. She didn't know why that was all of sudden, because she'd never had trouble sharing her most intimate secrets with Gretchen's son before, but now he had Alana and things were...different.

"How's my favorite girl?" Gretchen asked. Saedra nearly wept when she took a deep breath and inhaled the scent that was uniquely Gretchen. Roses. Always roses.

"I'm okay."

Gretchen gently set her back, her blue eyes scanning her face, her own eyes dimming. "Is my son's wedding stressing you out?"

Saedra tried to reassure the woman with a smile. "No. Just busy."

She didn't believe her. Then again, Gretchen had always known what she was thinking. "Well, I'm sure Alana and Trent appreciate all you're doing. You need to fill me in on everything, and to let me help you from here on out. I don't want you to collapse the day of the wedding."

She'd missed her cozy chats with Gretchen. When Trent had been out on the road, Saedra had been the one to look in on his mom. It'd been a weekly occurrence and now that she was face-to-face with Gretchen, she longed for one of their chats.

"I'll do that. Just let me finish up here and maybe we can get together later on."

The comforting hands fell away from her shoulders. "I'm going to take Alana into Reno for wedding dress shopping, so maybe after that. Just the two of us. Like old times."

The words made her want to cry all over again. "I'd like that."

"Well, okay, then."

She spent the rest of the day following up on last-minute details in Cabe's office above the barn, a place where she could watch the rental crew put the last few finishing touches on the tent, which had arrived early so they could give the ground beneath the parquet floor time to dry out. Next she confirmed with the florist that they were still willing to load their flowers on the same truck as everything else. Finally, she made sure their tables and chairs would be arriving, and a portable barbecue—one of the big guns—so she could roast enough meat for the entire wedding party. There would be seventy people, a small number compared to some of the weddings she'd catered in the past, but given that Alana and Trent had only been engaged for a couple of weeks, a fair amount of people. There was also one more thing she worked on, a surprise for Rana on Christmas morning.

Down below, she watched as Cabe shook hands with the rental crew, the tent looking like a mini ski chalet with its multifaceted roofline. She waited for him to tip his head back and peer up at her from beneath the brim of his hat. He knew where she was. To be honest she'd chosen the location on purpose. Away from the house. Free of inquiring minds such as Rana's and Alana's. Free of curious eyes such as Gretchen's and Trent's. Alas, all he did was turn toward the house.

Saedra slumped in disappointment.

They would have very few moments alone in the coming days. Gretchen would be staying in the big house. More guests would arrive tomorrow and the next day and they would fill the empty cabins. If they weren't staying in one of the ranch's rentals, then they would be staying in town or in their own horse trailer/living quarters on ranch property, which meant guests all over the place. In other words, chaos, and yet, there he went, off to the house, away from her.

She feared it wouldn't be the last time he walked away from her.

HE KNEW SHE WATCHED.

He forced himself to keep on walking. They needed

to keep up appearances. The last thing he wanted was for Rana to catch wind of their relationship. Granted, his teenage daughter had made it clear she liked Saedra and wanted them to get together, but he worried about the ramifications if things didn't work out. He didn't want to drag Rana through the ups and downs of a fledgling relationship, especially when he was still trying to figure things out on his own.

"Dad!" his daughter said the moment he walked in, Cabe turning to hang his hat by the front door. "Why aren't you up in the office with Saedra?"

He was in the middle of turning back to face her, but he froze, pretending to fiddle with the zipper of his jacket. "Did Saedra call down and ask to see me?" He tried to sound casual and vaguely disinterested.

"No, but I thought for sure you'd want a little more alone time with her before all heck breaks loose."

It took several deep breaths and the distraction of shrugging out of his jacket and hanging that, too, by the door before he felt comfortable enough to face her without giving the game away.

"Why would I want to be alone with her?"

His daughter did the teenage equivalent of rolling her eyes—a snort and a shake of her head—before saying, "Dad, I know you're seeing her. You were with her this morning."

It was all he could do not to let his mouth gape open.

"I don't know why you're trying to hide it. I think Saedra's great. I told you that the other day. And, honestly, it's about time."

"Wait, wait, wait," he said, lifting his hands. "It's not like that. We're just friends."

"Friends with benefits?"

"Rana!"

She grinned, motioning him into the kitchen. He didn't want to have this discussion, not with his daughter, but the girl was like a dog with a bone, and so he knew he fought a losing battle.

"Sit. We're going to talk."

Oh, great. A lecture from his fourteen-year-old daughter. He couldn't wait.

"There's nothing to talk about." He followed her into the kitchen just the same.

"She's beautiful, Dad." His daughter sat opposite him. "And that Stewart guy was all over her the other night at the campfire. You should snap her up before someone else does."

"I'm not interested in snapping *anyone* up."

Rana tipped her head down, clearly disbelieving. "No? Not even someone as beautiful as Saedra?"

"Saedra and I are friends," he said again. "We're both a little gun-shy. That's why we get along."

He hadn't thought of it that way, but now that he'd said the words he knew it was true. She understood what he was going through on a level he'd never encountered before.

"Do you think you could fall in love with her?"

Love?

"She'd make a *great* stepmother."

"What? No! It isn't like that."

The disappointment in his daughter's eyes made his stomach turn. Was she hoping he'd remarry? Did she want a new mom? Had she missed having a woman around that much? She'd had Alana.

"I *like* Saedra," he added. "She's a good friend."

"Then why are you sleeping with her?"

Dear God in heaven. "It's hard to explain."

"You always told me you should love someone before you sleep with them."

He felt as though he had dropped off the edge of an elevator shaft. "When you're older, it's different."

"Different how?"

"I told you, we're just friends." He was evading the question, he knew that, but damned if he knew what to say. "Saedra understands how the game is played."

"So this is a game to you?"

"No." Damn it. He hadn't wanted to go down this road with Rana. Not yet. Maybe not ever.

"Well, I think it's wrong. And I think you're wrong. I think you really do care about her. I think you're just telling me you don't because you're afraid, sort of like Alana was afraid to fall in love with Trent."

"Rana—"

"She's sweet and she's beautiful and she loves horses and she has a cat. You know how long I've wanted a cat. What more could you want?"

What more could *Rana* want?

He wanted someone to live on the ranch with him fulltime. Someone who wouldn't leave for weeks at a time to go chase her rodeo dreams. Someone who wasn't so damn beautiful that every time another man looked at her cross-eyed he wanted to beat that man down with his fists.

"I don't know what I want," he said honestly.

And there it was again, the disappointment in his daughter's eyes. She'd gotten her hopes up and here he was dashing them all. How much more would it hurt if he'd allowed things to get serious with Saedra right off the bat? If he'd told his daughter she might be the one? If he'd been free and easy about the whole relationship to the point that Rana had started to really care about

Saedra? It wasn't just himself that might get hurt, it was Rana, too.

"Maybe you should talk to her about it," Rana said.

It was too soon. Things had happened too fast. Damn it. For the first time since he'd slept with Saedra he wondered if it hadn't been a mistake.

Chapter Twenty

He never came up to the office. When she went to go find him an hour or so later, she was told by Rana that he'd run to town. There was something about the way the teenager looked at her that put Saedra on alert. It was as if she wanted to ask her something, but lacked the courage.

"What?" Saedra asked.

"Nothing," she replied, though her shoulders slumped as she climbed up the steps. "I'm going to go play with Ramses for a little bit." She disappeared.

What was going on?

After this morning she'd have thought Cabe would be well past avoiding her. Apparently not.

It didn't help that Alana called to tell her they would be out late. They were hitting Reno's shopping mall in a desperate last-ditch effort to find a wedding dress, and with the two-hour drive home, they wouldn't be back until near midnight. Saedra wished them luck, but she was disappointed to miss out on talking to Gretchen, especially as time ticked by and Cabe didn't return.

She finally went to bed, cuddling with Ramses, Rana having long since left the room, and Saedra wondering if Cabe would come to her that night as she climbed beneath the covers.

He didn't.

THE NEXT DAY made all the previous day seem peaceful. The wedding was in two days, which meant guests began to stream in, errands needed to be run. In all the chaos she nearly forgot about her role as best woman. She assumed she should have some sort of dinner for the bride and groom, and so there was that, too, to coordinate.

"You look plum wore out," Gretchen said when she found her in Cabe's office later that morning. The woman wore the same type of attire she'd worn for years—a fur-lined vest covering a long-sleeved shirt, one with a Western design across the front, and slim-fitted jeans. She had her long blond hair clipped back from each side of her face. "Honey, I think you need to go upstairs right now and take a nap."

"Gretchen, I'm not five years old."

"Not anymore, you're not," the woman said, coming up alongside of her and tucking an arm around her waist. "But you're still a daughter to me."

Gretchen, Alana and Trent hadn't gotten home until well after midnight, although Rana had told her they'd returned from Reno successful. Not only had they found Alana a dress, but they'd found two bridesmaid dresses they liked, too. All of the gowns were being altered this morning and then delivered later on today. Saedra had heard them come in, though she'd given in to sleep long before she'd heard Cabe return. For all she knew, he might not have come home at all.

"It's just been a crazy day," Saedra said, heading for the stairs. She'd left the seating chart in her room and she needed to make some changes now that she knew for certain who would be attending. "I still need to call the company delivering the wine and spirits, make sure the photographer is coming, confirm with the pastor who's officiating—"

"Let me help with that." Gretchen followed her up the steps. "You're doing too much."

"No, no, it's okay." When she reached the first landing she turned toward Cabe's bedroom door. It was closed.

"Saedra," Gretchen said, stepping in front of her. "What's wrong?"

Was she that obvious? "I need to get upstairs."

Gretchen followed, but Saedra had known she would, though it took every ounce of her self-control to act as if nothing was amiss when, in fact, her stomach burned as if on fire, every nerve in her body all but screaming, *Something is wrong.*

Gretchen knew it, too. The moment they were alone, Ramses dancing around her feet, Gretchen guided Saedra to the very seat where she'd sat and discussed Cabe with Alana not too long ago. Today it was warmer outside, and Saedra tipped her head back to the sunlight and let the rays warm her skin. She heard rather than saw Gretchen take a seat next to her.

"Spill."

"It's complicated."

"It has to do with Cabe, doesn't it?"

She opened her eyes, nearly blinded by sunlight, forcing herself to meet Gretchen's gaze. Ramses had jumped into the older woman's lap, the feline clearly thrilled to receive an unexpected visit from one of his favorite humans.

"Alana told me the two of you were dating," Gretchen added. "I think that's great, Saedra. I know you've been in a slump when it comes to dating."

Slump? That was an understatement. If they gave out awards for least likely to succeed in a relationship, she would win hands down.

"I don't think I'm doing so well with Cabe, either," she admitted.

"What? How's that possible. Alana was singing his praises yesterday and saying how much she hoped it worked out between the two of you."

Why was her mouth suddenly dry? She'd been wanting to talk to Gretchen about the whole situation since yesterday, but suddenly words failed her.

"Saedra?" Gretchen prompted.

Her whole body twitched. "I think I'm falling in love with him."

She saw Gretchen's eyes grow as wide as Ramses's when she accidentally stepped on him. "So soon?"

"I know," Saedra cried, shaking her head. "What's wrong with me? I should have kept things simple. Instead, I went and complicated matters by starting to care."

As she thought of the times she'd held him in her arms, of the way he held her that day and cried, she knew she did care. How could she not? That was the moment she'd started to fall, the moment when he'd totally exposed himself in a way she'd never experienced before, and it had melted her heart.

Gretchen touched her leg, garnering her attention. "That's the problem, I think," she said softly. "You so desperately want to find love, my dear. Sometimes you don't think things through."

"Oh, I thought this through." She inhaled because for some foolish reason she wanted to cry. "I thought about it a lot. I even went out with someone else last week. Cabe was furious."

Gretchen frowned. "You didn't sleep with that man, too, did you?"

"No! Of course not. I'm not *that* messed up."

"I know, I know," Gretchen said, her blue eyes kind.

"You've got the biggest heart of anyone I know. Cabe would be a fool not to see that."

"He does care for me." She nodded her head to emphasize her point. "I just don't know if he could ever love me."

"Why not?"

Saedra leaned forward. "Why didn't you ever remarry?"

Gretchen seemed startled by the question. She pet Ramses for a moment before saying, "Why, I guess because I didn't see the need."

"Do you love Paul?"

"I do."

"The same way you loved Richard?"

The hand petting Ramses froze. Saedra could tell the question took her by surprise. "I don't think I could ever love someone like that again."

Saedra nodded. "I think Cabe's in the same boat."

For the first time, Gretchen seemed to understand. She tipped her head sideways, her eyes full of concern, mouth tipping down a bit. "That is a problem, then, isn't it?"

So much of a problem that Saedra's stomach felt as if it were at a constant simmer, burning, her heart pounding as she felt the need to run. "What if he can't love me?"

She hadn't meant the words to sound so full of anguish, but she knew they did because Gretchen's eyes softened even more. "Then he's a damn fool." She leaned close. "But you don't know for a fact that he can't, so try not to worry. You'll see. Things will work out."

Saedra wasn't certain they would. Not at all.

HE KNEW HE behaved like a coward.

Instead of speaking with Saedra about his concerns he managed to avoid her for the rest of the day, but he consoled himself with the thought that it wasn't really his fault. He felt like he was at Disneyland. His phone began to ring off the hook. People dropped by the ranch to see Alana and Trent. A few of them had been given the go-ahead to park their trucks and trailers on ranch property, so he had to show them where to park. He damn near missed Saedra's text message informing him that a rehearsal dinner had been set for the following day at a local bar and grill.

By the time dinner rolled around it was a full-on party, so many guests having arrived and then staying for a while that he felt lucky to catch a glimpse of her chatting with someone who looked vaguely familiar. She glanced over and smiled at him, and Cabe was momentarily distracted by her off-white sweater, a cowl neckline dropping low over her back and exposing her soft flesh, but she immediately turned her attention back to the wedding guest. When he blinked, she was gone, and when he stepped off to find her, Alana jumped in front of him and asked him if he'd mind getting more wine for their guests.

So he continued to play peekaboo with her for the next hour. He might never have had a moment alone with her if he hadn't spotted someone picking up and shaking Kimberly's snow globe, his heart pitching in his chest for a second in fear they might drop it. They didn't and the first opportunity he got he scooped the thing up, determined to stash it in his den.

Saedra was there.

He almost backed out of the room, but the smile she gave him held him in place, though he could see it was strained.

"Hey," she said softly.

She'd been looking at something. A seating chart.

"Why aren't you enjoying the party?" he asked.

"There wasn't supposed to be a party tonight." She released a breath. "I still have things to do. Thought I had the seating chart all figured out, but then we had a few more last-minute RSVPs."

He nodded, glanced down at the snow globe he held in his hands, the snow dancing around inside, the golden carousel pole catching the light. It occurred to him then that this was his first Christmas party since Kimberly died. Such parties used to be an annual occurrence....

"Did you need to stash that in here?"

He'd been lost there for a moment. Her words brought him back to the present.

"Yeah." He moved into the room. "I'm just afraid someone might break it."

She nodded. "Good call." She watched as he set the glass ornament down on his desk. "I know it would be tough on you to lose such an important memento."

Why did he have a feeling she wasn't talking about just the snow globe. "It was her favorite."

"I know," she said softly.

Again, he had a feeling there was more to her words than met the eye.

"It would break Rana's heart if it broke."

And now he was speaking with double meanings because he wasn't talking about the snow globe. As he stood in front of her, as he looked into her beautiful eyes, he knew what he had to do. Not just for Saedra's sake, but for Rana, too. And for his sake, as well, because he'd been filled with so much panic at the thought of someone breaking one of Kimberly's treasures that he knew he wasn't ready to let go.

"I promise to keep a close eye on it."

"Thank you."

Leave, Cabe. Now. Before you do something impul-

sive like pull her to her feet and give in to the urge to kiss her bare back.

Sex.

They had that in spades, this wild attraction. Even now he fought it, but Rana was right. He had no business messing around with her unless he loved her. And he didn't love her.

Did he?

He immediately shied away from the thought, appalled at himself that he could even consider the notion. Kimberly had been his one true love.

"Cabe." He watched her struggle for a moment, his heart suddenly skipping in his chest like a rock on the surface of a pond. "I want you to know how much I appreciate all that you've done." She blinked quickly, almost as if she were on the verge of tears. "For Alana and Trent, I mean. You're a good man."

No, he wasn't. He was an ass. Why else was he forcing himself to stand still when, clearly, she wanted him to pull her into his arms? He could read the longing in her eyes, could see how hard it was for her to keep it together.

"It's the least I could do."

"I know," she said quickly. She looked down for a moment, blinked, then met his gaze. "Kimberly was a lucky woman."

She was saying goodbye.

"Saedra—"

She stood. "I should get going."

"Saedra, wait." He grabbed her hand as she passed by. She didn't want to turn and face him, he could tell, so he stepped in front of her. "I'm sorry."

She flinched, but she didn't let him see the pain in her eyes, and he knew she was hurt.

"Sorry about what?" she asked, lifting her chin.

Kissing you. Holding you. Leading you to believe things would be different.

"Asking you to do so much." Now he was the one who wasn't saying what he really meant. "The wedding and all," he tacked on, still unable to be honest with her.

What a jerk he turned out to be.

"It's okay," she said. "I knew what I was getting into."

His hands flexed. He wanted to reach for her, knew he couldn't.

"You're an amazing woman, Saedra," he said, echoing the tone she'd used earlier. "One day you'll make someone a great wife."

He saw her inhale sharply, saw her blink a few more times, and he would never, ever forget the way she lifted her chin, the way she held his gaze, when she said, "I know."

And then she was gone.

Chapter Twenty-One

She didn't want to wake up.

But Ramses wouldn't let her sleep. She groaned as a soft cat's paw batted her face.

"Stop it," she muttered.

That prompted a meow. She opened an eye. Ramses scowled. She scowled right back.

Two more days.

That's all she had to stick it out for—one more night. She would leave after the wedding tomorrow instead of New Year's Eve as she'd originally planned. First, however, there was the damn rehearsal dinner. Yet another party. She didn't think she could stand being near Cabe and yet not being able to touch him.

You did fall in love with him, didn't you?

Last night, when he'd come into the study, she'd known instantly she had. The sight of him carrying that globe, knowing how much it meant to him, seeing the way he cradled it so tenderly. She loved him.

And he loved someone else.

It was ironic, really. Of all the men she'd dated over the years, many of them total losers, none of them had been in love with another woman. That lovely little heartache she'd never suffered before. Yeah, well, the joke was on her because the woman she'd lost Cabe to wasn't even alive anymore.

"All right, fine," she told Ramses, shoving the covers back so quickly the cat jumped away in surprise. "I'll feed you."

Ten minutes later she'd pulled on a dark blue sweater and a pair of jeans, a glance outside the window revealing another nice day outside, though she suspected it would be cold, probably as cold as her heart right now.

It was Christmas Eve.

Tomorrow Alana and Trent would get married. She should be happy for them, and she was; it just didn't feel like Christmas.

It smelled like Christmas, though, when she opened her door after patting Ramses goodbye. The scent of the tree wafted all the way up the stairs, getting stronger the closer to the bottom floor she got. Was he in the kitchen?

No.

But someone else was, the sight of him bringing her up short.

"Well, if it isn't my favorite little cowgirl," said the man, removing his cowboy hat and tossing it on a countertop to his left. "I was wondering if you were going to make an appearance. Thought you'd died."

"Mac." Her dimly beating heart suddenly kicked into gear. Trent's roping partner was as near and dear to her as Trent himself.

Thank God it was Mac. Not Cabe.

She was in Mac's arms before she'd taken two steps into the kitchen. He hugged her so hard she couldn't breathe, but when he moved back, she wouldn't let him, her arms wrapping around his big frame. Mac was six-foot-plus of beef and brawn, and she needed every ounce of his strength right now. She squeezed him back as hard as she could.

"Whoa." The minute she released him, he set her back. His brown eyes were like a bar code scan, flickering over her face, registering the fact that something wasn't right. "You okay?"

"Fine." She took a deep breath. "Just tired. Been crazy the past few days."

That was certainly true.

"Well, sit down and have some breakfast. Rana here is a great cook."

She hadn't even seen Rana sitting there, the teenager staring at her with a troubled look on her face, too. "There's pancakes warming in the oven." She motioned with her chin toward the stove. "Bacon is in the microwave." She frowned. "You look tired."

"I am tired. Ramses kept me up."

That and replaying her conversation with Cabe over and over again in her mind. She'd never forget the look on his face as he'd all but kissed her goodbye on the cheek and sent her on her merry way.

One day you'll make someone a great wife.

Just not him.

"Eat, eat." Mac patted the table until she sat down.

Truth was, she didn't have much of an appetite, but she took a seat, anyway. In a moment she had a plate of pancakes in front of her—compliments of Mac—even a glass of orange juice. She passed on the bacon. At least she could pretend to gum the pancakes.

"Okay, so spill it," Mac said. "What's wrong?"

Next to Trent Mac was her closest friend. She wanted— oh, how she wanted—to unburden herself, but Rana stared at her, too, and the last thing she wanted was for the teenage girl to know what was going on.

"Does this have something to do with my dad?"

"Cabe?" Mac asked, appearing curious. "You two still at each other's throats?"

She almost snorted, the words so far from the truth they made her want to laugh. "We're getting along fine." Which was true.

Rana didn't buy it. The teenager must be incredibly intuitive because she eyed her like an adult would a child suspected of lying.

"Then why aren't you scarfing down your pancakes like you usually do?" Mac asked.

"Because I don't have time to eat." She pushed back from the table and stood. "Really."

"Sit down."

Mac's words brooked no argument, but the big man didn't scare her. She bent and kissed him on the cheek. "I'll see you later."

"Whoa, whoa…wait."

She couldn't. She just couldn't stick around. She had a few errands to run, and she planned to do them alone. Being in the house felt depressing. All those decorations, every one of them a reminder of Kimberly. The "other" woman.

She had her keys in her hand before she knew it, her jacket grabbed from a stand by the front door, Mac still calling her name, but she suddenly needed to leave.

Cabe was outside.

He was coming into the house and just the sight of him made everything inside of her still and then erupt like a shaken soda.

"Good morning," he said, breath misting as he spoke.

"Morning." She brushed past him while barely looking him in the eyes. She'd gotten the message loud and clear last night. They were done.

She spent the rest of the day running last-minute errands and conferring with Alana and Trent on any other problems, such as the fact that they'd forgotten to buy Alana ivory panty hose to go with her new wedding dress, and bobby pins, too, and Trent forgot underarm deodorant. Then, when she returned, she and Rana had to set up the tables and chairs and then got to work on the centerpieces—tiny manzanita branches that had been painted white and made to look like tiny trees dripped in crystals—each one taking a half hour to decorate. Then there was the tulle to be draped around the inside, and the Christmas lights, and the heaters tested... When next she looked up, the inside of the tent had been transformed and it was time to rehearse for the wedding.

"Oh, you guys! It looks *so* great."

Alana stood at the entrance to the tent, hand on her heart, eyes wide.

"Do you like it, Alana?" Rana asked. "I think it looks fantastic."

"It's like the inside of a fairy-tale castle." Alana's voice was full of wonder. "I can't believe you did all this in the amount of time you had."

"I know, right?" Rana sounded so excited it made Saedra smile for the first time all day. "I can't wait until tomorrow."

Alana pulled Rana into her arms, the two of them hugging and then drawing back and spinning around to look, arm and arm. Saedra had to look away. Her smile faded. She envied Alana. There. She'd admitted it. She'd captured the heart of a good man. She had Rana, too, and a future mother-in-law who would always love her. Saedra would never have those things.

"If you guys are going to change before we rehearse, you better do it now." Alana pulled her cell phone from her pocket, checked the time. "Pastor Bob will be here in a half hour. Cabe's already got the fire going outside. We're going to grill some steaks, and I'm sure we'll end up with a bunch of people around the fire. You know how it is."

Change? Should she?

Yes.

Tonight would be her last night at the ranch. Come hook or crook, she would leave after the wedding, that she vowed.

FOR THE TENTH time Cabe snapped the lid of the long jewelry box closed, the necklace inside disappearing from view, his eyes lifting to the picture of Kimberly and Rana that he kept on his dresser.

You would approve, wouldn't you, Kimberly?

He knew she would. He hadn't talked to Rana about what he wanted to do, but he knew she wouldn't mind, and so he tucked the box inside his jacket pocket. Five minutes later he stepped into the chilly dusk, everything outside tinged red by a setting sun. Tomorrow would be cold, too, but the heaters should keep their guests comfortable. The wedding was scheduled for three, late enough in the afternoon to have warmed a bit, but not so late that guests would be cold when they arrived.

"There he is," Alana announced.

He took a moment to take it all in. The roofline gave the place the look of an actual building. The arena sand had been completely covered by a parquet floor. Soft lights shed a subtle glow over all the decorations. Cabe was stunned by the job Saedra and Rana had done.

"Looks good, doesn't it?" Alana just about skipped as she came forward. "I couldn't believe it when I saw it."

"Looks good." He caught Trent's eyes, nodding to the

man who would soon be the husband of his closest friend. "I was hoping I could borrow your fiancée for a minute."

"Sure," Trent said.

The man seemed to realize Cabe wanted a moment alone with his future wife because he winked before turning to leave.

Alana didn't wait for Trent to be out of the tent before she pounced. "What's going on with you and Saedra?"

He tried to act surprised, knew he failed, but didn't want to get into it with her. "Nothing." He pulled the jewelry box from his jacket. "I wanted to give you this."

"What do you mean, nothing? The poor woman looks like she's been kicked in the teeth. You break up with her or something?"

"No." It was the truth. It'd been more of a mutual thing, he reasoned out. "Everything's fine. We're still good friends."

"With benefits?"

Good Lord. What was with everyone? "Just because we're friends doesn't mean we have to sleep together. Look at you and me."

It was true and Alana knew it, but she also knew there was more to the story than he let on, not that he gave her a chance to probe.

"Here." He held the velvet box out. "Been wanting to give this to you for some time now."

She stared up at him questioningly as she took the velvet-covered box. "What is it?"

"Open it up."

She did, slowly, her eyes widening and her mouth dropping open for a moment before she met his gaze again. "Oh, Cabe, this is beautiful. Was it Kimberly's?"

He nodded. He'd bought the sapphire-and-diamond pendant for one of their anniversaries. She'd only ever worn it on special occasions so the diamonds still sparkled and the gold still shone like it was new.

"Something blue," he said.

She looked about ready to cry. "Thanks, Cabe."

"What you got there?"

It was Trent's voice, but it wasn't just Trent who came inside. Trent had found the pastor, Saedra, Rana, Mac and Gretchen—the whole wedding party.

"What's that?" Rana asked.

Alana's eyes darted to Saedra before she said, "Your mother's necklace." She tugged the girl's ponytail. "Something blue."

She showed it to Rana, who gushed, "I remember that." She smiled up at her dad. "That's perfect."

"You think so?"

"Yup. And she's going to borrow mom's veil, too, so she'll have something old and the dress will be something new."

"Sounds like you're all set, then," Pastor Bob said, a big burly man who could match Mac pound for pound. The man was a familiar sight on the rodeo circuit according to Trent, often leading the crowd in a prayer, his black hat the old-fashioned kind with a low crown and a narrow brim. "You ready to do a run-through or two?"

Alana nodded, all smiles, though it seemed to dim a bit when she spotted Saedra hanging back a bit. "Let's do it," she said, her smile returning when she took Trent's hand.

It would be a simple ceremony and so didn't take long to get organized. Gretchen would stand in as father of the bride and would walk Alana down the aisle. The rest of them had to go through the process of learning their parts. A string quartet would play tomorrow so Pastor Bob went over the music selection, which would cue when they were supposed to start walking. Once at the altar Cabe would stand by Alana as "man of honor" and Saedra would be next to Trent—the other two, Rana and Mac, would stand on the edges. That was the simple part. Not so simple was listening to Alana and Trent's vows, the memory of the time when he'd spoken his own vows causing emotions to wreak havoc inside his already scavenged mind.

He tried to keep it to himself. But Saedra noticed.

He had no idea how she'd spotted the telltale signs of his distress. His face was in profile, his gaze firmly trained upon Trent and Alana, but she knew. Perhaps by the tension in his shoulders. Maybe she'd noticed the way his hands clenched and unclenched. Then, too, she might have spotted the rigidity in his jaw. All he knew was that the moment he caught her eye, she mouthed the words, "You okay?"

No.

But he nodded nonetheless.

Hang in there, her eyes told him.

He did his best, smiled at the appropriate time, moved around when asked, then he stood through the whole thing again, and by the time they were done, it was all he could do not to bolt through the door.

"Who's hungry?" Mac asked.

"I am," said Rana. "Starving."

"Me, too," said Alana.

"I was going to make a potato salad," said Gretchen.

"Mmm, Mom's famous potato salad," Trent said with a wide smile. "Pastor Bob, you staying for dinner? I think we'll have plenty of food."

"He might as well," interjected Alana. "I suspect some of our campers will be joining us, too."

They all moved out en masse, Cabe grateful everyone seemed to have their mind on food and not on him. Everyone but Saedra, that is. She stepped in front of him before he could leave the tent.

"You going to be okay?"

She appeared so concerned and so genuinely distressed on his behalf that for a moment he had a hard time remembering why it was he'd convinced himself it could never work between the two of them.

"Fine."

She tipped her head a bit to the side, blond hair rippling over one shoulder like a horse's mane. She looked beautiful in her thick sweater. More beautiful than any woman he'd seen in a long, long time.

"It was nice what you did." She glanced away for a second. "Giving that necklace to Alana. It'll look beautiful on her tomorrow."

It'd looked beautiful on Kimberly. He remembered the expression on her face when she'd opened it on Christmas.

Christmas.

He felt his hands begin to shake. "I should go."

"Cabe, wait."

He'd expected her to be angry with him. To stare up at him with accusation in her eyes, or maybe disappointment, but she didn't. No. Instead, she grabbed his hand and for a long time said nothing.

"I told myself I would ignore you tonight." God help him, she suddenly sounded on the verge of tears. "That I would laugh and flirt and make you jealous." She looked up at him with wide blue eyes, so wide he could practically see himself in them. "But I can't do that because I understand. I know all too well what it's like to lose someone. First my dad, then my mom...sort of. There have been other people along the way, people I never really loved, I know that now, but still, it's never easy. You lost a *wife,* your best friend, a lover, not to mention your brother, too. I can't imagine what that must feel like." She squeezed his hand. "I want you to know that no matter what's happened between us, no matter how much I hoped things would work out differently, I will always, *always* be your friend."

So completely humbled by her words did he feel that he didn't know what to say.

"You're a good man, Cabe Jensen." She reached up and kissed him lightly on the cheek. "Be happy."

Chapter Twenty-Two

She cried herself to sleep.

It was stupid, really; she'd made her peace with Cabe. She shouldn't be upset. She should be happy that she could face him and not feel totally uncomfortable or disappointed.

She lied to herself.

Because the moment she opened her eyes she knew today would only ever end up being painful.

"Merry Christmas to me," she mumbled to herself.

It had dawned a beautiful day, one of those mornings that was so spectacularly beautiful, Saedra wanted to cry. Of course, she couldn't do that. The last thing she needed was Alana or Gretchen or Rana spotting the remnants of her tears—and they would—so she steeled herself against the coming day, warned herself that there might be a moment when she would be forced to hold it together.

That moment came far more quickly than she would have expected. She'd been busy most of the morning. Gifts had arrived for the wedding party, the meat that needed to be seasoned and slow-roasted, the wedding favors had to be set out, and she'd had to run into town to pick up Rana's Christmas present. The list went on, so when she looked up and spotted Trent in a black cowboy hat standing at the foot of the stairs in a Western-style suit, at first she didn't know who it was.

"Why aren't you dressed yet?"

"Trent!" She glanced at her cell phone. "Crud. I didn't realize it was so late."

She hadn't wanted to think about the ticking clock. The fact that soon Trent and Alana would be married and she would be out of reasons to stick around.

"I'll be right back." She started to dash up the steps.

"Wait." Trent's words had her pausing on the steps. "I came in here looking for you, to give you this."

He held a box. Lord, how had she not noticed him holding something? Was she that distracted?

"Trent, no, you didn't have to get me something for Christmas." Especially since she hadn't gotten him anything. He had everything he wanted, she'd assumed, and how do you shop for a man like that? "Really. Put it away for next year."

She started up the steps again.

"Saedra, it's not a Christmas present. It's your best woman present."

Best woman present? She faced him again. "Are you kidding?"

"It's a tradition." He held out the box.

Saedra moved down the steps, taking the box from his outstretched hands.

"Actually," he said, "we were kind of hoping you'd wear them today. Under your dress."

What the heck—

She ripped the silver foil off the outside of the box. There was a name stamped onto the lid of the box, one spelled out in gold-leaf ink and that seemed familiar. She pulled on the lid.

Spurs.

She almost laughed, but a gasp preempted the reaction, because she'd never seen such a beautiful set in her life. "Oh, Trent, they're stunning."

They'd had her name carved into the sides, gold filigree and raised silver flowers scrolled around its edges. A date was etched into the shank—Trent and Alana's wedding date—and it made her want to cry.

"I love them," she said, clutching the box to her.

"Good. Cabe got the male version of them. Rana and Mac got a pair, too." He smiled, his face suddenly serious. "You've been my best friend for more years than I can remember, Saedra. I hope you know how much it means to me to have you here."

"I do."

She was in his arms before she could take another breath, and it was all she could do not to break down. Everything was just so messed up. She'd gone and done something stupid. She'd fallen for a man who didn't want her. Stupid, stupid, stupid.

He drew back, frowning. "I hope those are happy tears."

"They are." She sniffed. "Of course they are."

His frown turned into a smile. "Good. See you outside, then? The photographer's already here."

"Okay, good." How did she do it? How did she sound so chipper when all she wanted to do was curl up into a little ball and sob. "See you out there."

She dashed away and up the stairs before he could say another word.

"Tell Rana we're ready to go, too," he called out after her. "I'm off to find my mother. She's guarding Alana in case I get some wild and crazy urge to jump my future wife in her wedding dress before the ceremony." He shook his head. "God forbid."

Rana.

"Will do."

She'd forgotten about the girl's gift. Well, not really forgotten, but she needed to give it to her before the wedding started because she'd be gone the minute Trent and Alana said, "I do." If she didn't get out of here soon she'd go crazy. All of it—the Christmas decorations, the wedding decorations, Trent's happy face—was just too painful a reminder of what could never be.

"Rana?" she called, stopping before the teenager's closed door across the landing from Cabe's room. Was he in there, too? He must be out; otherwise, Trent would have said something.

"Just a second."

The door swung wide. For the second time that morning Saedra found herself close to tears, but this time for a different reason. "Oh, Rana, you look beautiful."

"Do I?" the teenager asked, turning sideways so she could admire the long-sleeved purple dress. She touched her hair, which she'd piled atop her head in a way that looked entirely too grown up for Saedra's peace of mind. "It's not too, you know, low cut?"

The floor-length dress was long-sleeved and not the least bit risqué. "You look great."

Saedra had a dress just like it up in her room. She'd tried it on last night, surprised to find it fit like a glove considering how quickly it'd been altered.

"Why aren't *you* dressed?" Rana frowned.

"I was going to do that right now, but first I have a surprise I want to give you."

"Oh, oh, oh!" Rana exclaimed, spotting the box in her hands. "Did you give me spurs, too?"

Saedra glanced down. "No." She found herself smiling despite the fact that she would have sworn such a thing would be impossible a few minutes ago. "I have something else. Come on up to my room."

Rana needed no second urging, but when she walked, she made a noise that had Saedra drawing up short.

"What's on your feet?"

"The spurs." Rana lifted the edge of her dress, which revealed cowboy boots. "I'm wearing them today."

She wanted to laugh. She wanted to cry. She wanted to pull the teenager into her arms. It would have been so great to get to know Rana better. She was exactly the type of girl she'd always hoped to have. Smart. Kind. Horse crazy. Cat crazy, too, speaking of which...

"Come on." But she had to dash away tears as she climbed the steps.

"I have something for you for Christmas, too," Rana said from behind her. "It's nothing much, but I hope you like it."

"I'm sure I will," Saedra said, opening the door to her room. A tiny little meow instantly greeted her. She'd worried Ramses might cause trouble, but she should have known better. Her cat sat on the windowsill pretending to be indifferent to the room's tiny intruder.

"Merry Christmas," Saedra said, scooping up the kitten and handing it to Rana.

She'd rendered her speechless. Or maybe not. Her mouth opened and closed a few times. It took Saedra a moment to realize she was on the verge of tears.

"For me?" she said, cuddling the orange tabby, another Peke-faced Persian, up to her chin.

"For you."

Saedra let the tears fall. She might not be around after today, but Cabe would always have a reminder of her at the ranch, although that's not why she'd done it. She'd

given the girl a kitten because she so clearly adored
Ramses and deserved a cat of her own.

"Oh, Saedra." Yup. Those were tears. "Thank you
so much."

They hugged, Saedra closing her eyes against more
tears. She adored the girl. No doubt about it.

"Now, listen," she said, drawing back. "If your dad
gives you any grief you send him to me."

"He won't."

"He better not because if he does, I'll drag him out
behind the barn. Just promise me you'll take good care
of him."

"I will."

"Good." She wiped at her eyes. "Okay, go, I have to
get dressed."

"Wait. I have something for you, too." She was gone,
kitten still cuddled in her arms, before Saedra could tell
her to give her the gift later. She was back almost instantly, though.

"Here."

Rana handed her a flat package wrapped in bright
green paper.

A frame.

Inside was a picture of her and Cabe, riding, the two of
them smiling. They were up on the ridge, the hills in the
background, steam rising from their horses' coats. She
remembered the moment well. Cabe had just mentioned
something about the ranch, and how easy it'd been to hide
away, and she'd smiled up at him and agreed. Rana must
have taken the photo at that exact moment.

"It's perfect," she said softly.

"I had hoped…" Rana's voice faltered for a moment.
"I was sort of hoping you and Dad could work things out.
You know. Start dating or something."

Her lips had begun to tremble and she had to work so hard not to cry. "Me, too."

Rana had spotted the tears in her eyes, and her own eyes filled with sorrow. "He's an idiot."

Deep breath. She inhaled. *Okay, take another.*

"No." Her voice sounded clogged with tears. "He loved your mother very much."

Rana nodded. "I would have loved getting to know you."

Her lips trembled ever harder. "Me, too." Breathe. "Okay, go," she said softly. "I need to get dressed before Trent starts yelling at me again."

Rana didn't move. "My dad's blind," she said softly.

Or a fool, Saedra thought to herself, giving the girl a gentle hug, mindful of the kitten.

"I won't argue with that." She tapped her on the rear. "Now, go."

THEY TOOK PICTURES.

Cabe tried not to gawk at the sight of Saedra in her purple gown, standing in front of a row of bushes near Alana's home. The washed silk fabric clung to her every curve. She'd piled her hair up high, the chill in the air turning her cheeks a color that nearly matched the roses in her bridal bouquet, her face so perfectly beautiful he had to look away.

"Good-looking wedding party, yeah?" Mac said, clapping Cabe on the back.

"Oh, yeah."

They stood at a distance, watching. Alana posed for the photographer with what looked like snow at her feet, but was really a clever backdrop. His best friend had pulled her hair back off her face, the style emphasizing the heartlike shape, her light blue eyes heavily outlined.

She looked beautiful in a no-frills gown that hugged her slender waist. He'd told her so when he'd first seen her... but Saedra outshone her.

"Why aren't you wearing your spurs?" Mac asked, staring at the black boots that matched his suit.

"Forgot."

He'd been frazzled all morning. After last night's conversation with Saedra he should have felt better about things, less stressed about having hurt her feelings, or that she hated him. Instead, the words that best described him this morning were...*on edge*.

"You need me to run and go get them for you?"

It looked like they had a few moments before the photographer needed them. "No. I'll do it."

He dashed into the back of the house, intending to head straight for his bedroom, but he was brought up short when he glimpsed inside his den. A ray of sunlight beamed through the window, the bright light falling perfectly and squarely on the snow globe he'd left there yesterday.

Kimberly.

His feet turned toward the room, though he didn't remember making the decision to go in there. When he glanced around, he couldn't figure out where the beam came from. The window was in the wrong direction, which meant it had to be refracting off something. What?

He looked around, curious, and if he were honest, his hair was standing on end. It was as if a spotlight shone down on the globe. When he followed the length of the beam it led upward, toward a shelf behind his desk, and a silver box.

The box.

Good Lord. He'd forgotten about it. He'd stashed it

up high after Kimberly's death. Hadn't thought about it since. Hadn't wanted to think about it.

Once again his feet seemed to have a mind of their own. He had to use a chair to reach it. He worried for a moment he might fall and break his neck. He didn't. The heavy silver box slid easily into his hand, the metal cold, dust filling the air.

He knew what was inside. Rana's baby teeth. A letter Rana had written to Santa when she was five, in crayon. And their wedding rings.

He'd put them there so he wouldn't have to bump into them. Ever. Yet here he was, gently opening the box, and peering down at three gold rings, one with a diamond— for Rana when she got older—and one far larger than the others. His. A simple gold band. He picked it up.

If removed, alarm will sound.

He remembered laughing when he'd first read the inscription all those years ago. Now he smiled. Leave it to Kimberly to come up with something clever. His had the more generic *'Til death do us part* inside.

"Dad?"

He set the ring back, snapped the lid closed just as Rana found him in the study.

"We need you outside."

"Be right there."

Rana didn't wait for a response, which was good. He didn't immediately put the box away. Instead, he stared at it.

'Til death do us part.

The words haunted him.

Death had parted them.

The beam of light on the snow globe was gone. Cabe told himself it hadn't really been a sign, but as he left the study, he wondered.

Saedra wasn't outside when he returned. It was the men's turn with the bride, Mac informed him. The ladies were done. Well, all but Saedra. She was off to go find Trent for her photos with him.

He didn't see Saedra again until it was time for Alana to walk down the aisle. She'd already taken her position next to Trent as "best woman." She smiled at him when their gazes connected, guests beginning to sit at the round tables between them, a string quartet playing soft music. Cabe had to force himself to back away.

Alana waited for him off to the side, out of sight of the guests, his daughter picking at an invisible speck of lint or something on Alana's wedding dress, Trent's mother standing nearby and looking every bit as anxious as the bride.

"You ready for this?" he asked Alana, but he included Gretchen in his smile.

"Never been more ready in my life," Alana said.

The music changed. It was their cue to start walking.

Rana shot up. "See you after."

Yes, after. But he didn't want to go inside. He didn't want to face what was coming. The wedding vows. The happiness on the bride's and groom's faces. The memories.

Somehow he walked. He didn't remember making his way down the aisle. Didn't look at Saedra or Trent or Mac or his daughter. He felt numb, physically numb, as the music changed yet again. The guests rose. Alana stood at the entrance. Somehow his gaze became entangled in Saedra's, and just as it had the day before, her gaze soothed him.

He didn't look away as Alana and Trent took their place, hardly heard a word as they began to exchange

vows, couldn't take his eyes off the kindness and understanding in her eyes.

'Til death do us part.

He thought the words were in his mind again until he
realized Trent and Alana were exchanging rings.

"I do," he heard Alana say.

Trent vowed to love and honor and cherish Alana next.
It hit him then, what Kimberly had been trying to tell
him earlier, because there could be little doubt that moment in the study had been a sign.

'Til death do us part.

Trent spoke the words this time.

Cabe had spoken them, too, once upon a time. He'd
loved and honored and cherished Kimberly, just as he
knew Trent would Alana. But now things were different—that's what she'd been trying to tell him. He'd honored his part of the bargain, now it was time to move on.

He heard the audience cheer, realized Trent and Alana
had been told it was okay to kiss, but the tears in his eyes
weren't out of happiness for his best friend and her new
husband, though he was happy for them. No, the tears
were for him, and for Saedra, and for anyone else who'd
ever lost a spouse.

Time to move on.

Had Rana spoken the words? He looked around, but
his daughter was beaming in Alana and Trent's direction.

No. That hadn't been Rana. That had been Kimberly's voice.

"Ladies and gentlemen, I'd like to introduce—"

"Wait!"

It was one of those weird moments when you hadn't
realized you were going to speak…until you'd already
spoken. Suddenly everyone stared in his direction. Sud-

denly, the tent had gone quiet. Suddenly, Trent and Alana had turned to face him.

"I just…"

Alana's eyes were wide. She glanced at Trent. Her new husband seemed as perplexed as Alana.

"I just want to say something before we, ah, before we all get up to congratulate the bride and groom."

"Dad," his daughter whispered. *"What are you doing?"*

He lifted a hand, hoping to silently shush her. "As most of you know, I was married once before."

He caught Alana's gaze and in that moment he saw her eyes widen. Did she know what he was about to do? She was his best friend—a bona fide mind reader at times— so maybe she did.

"It was a great marriage." He glanced down at his empty ring finger. "The best." He turned to Saedra. "I never thought I could find that kind of love again. But I was wrong."

"Dad?" Rana asked softly.

"Quiet, squirt, while your dad apologizes to the woman he loves," Alana said, shooting him an encouraging smile.

Someone gasped. Saedra. She stared at him, a hand covering her mouth in disbelief, the look on her face making him smile. For once, she was speechless. Who would have thought.

"I've been a plumb-ass fool," he told her.

"Yes, you have," his daughter echoed.

He shot Rana a look meant to warn her to be quiet, but that clearly failed miserably because she stuck her tongue out at him just before a smile broke out on her face, one so big that Cabe knew he'd made the right choice.

"Saedra," he said, moving to stand in front of her. She still had her hand over her mouth. "You're the only woman in the world who could ever understand me. Whose heart is so big there's room to love my daughter, too."

Tears poured down her face. She was trembling. Her whole body had started to shake.

"I love you. I don't know when it happened, but it did, and I can't stand the thought of you thinking I don't for one minute longer."

"Cabe," he heard her whisper softly.

"So before we let Alana and Trent run off to live their own happily ever after, I was wondering if I could ask you a question, here, in front of the people we love, with Alana and Trent's permission, of course."

His best friend and her new husband nodded. "Of course."

He got down on a knee, but not before pulling her hand away from her mouth. Saedra moaned, but not in pain. No, he heard the joy in that sound, the pure happiness.

"Saedra Robbins," he asked. "Will you marry me?"

More tears fell down her face, her lips lifting into a smile. "Yes."

"Thank you, God!" Rana yelled.

The audience clapped; Alana and Trent rushed forward. Saedra started to full-on cry. Rana jumped up and down. Cabe absorbed it all as he slowly stood. It was a moment he knew he would never forget, not in his entire life.

He pulled Saedra into his arms. Holding her, feeling the peace fill his soul, he knew he'd made the right choice.

"Are you sure?" she whispered.

He drew back and looked into her eyes. "Never been more sure about anything in my life."

Three days later, after one of the longest after-wedding

parties in the history of northern California, he proved it to her as, in front of the same group of family and friends, he slipped a ring onto Saedra's finger. This time he took a page from Kimberly's book when he had Saedra's ring inscribed.

One-night stands can last forever.
And theirs certainly did.

* * * * *

REQUEST YOUR FREE BOOKS!
2 FREE NOVELS PLUS 2 FREE GIFTS!

◆HARLEQUIN®

American ★ *Romance*®

LOVE, HOME & HAPPINESS

YES! Please send me 2 FREE Harlequin® American Romance® novels and my 2 FREE gifts (gifts are worth about $10). After receiving them, if I don't wish to receive any more books, I can return the shipping statement marked "cancel." If I don't cancel, I will receive 4 brand-new novels every month and be billed just $4.74 per book in the U.S. or $5.24 per book in Canada. That's a savings of at least 14% off the cover price! It's quite a bargain! Shipping and handling is just 50¢ per book in the U.S. and 75¢ per book in Canada.* I understand that accepting the 2 free books and gifts places me under no obligation to buy anything. I can always return a shipment and cancel at any time. Even if I never buy another book, the two free books and gifts are mine to keep forever.

154/354 HDN F4YN

Name _____ (PLEASE PRINT) _____

Address _____ Apt. # _____

City _____ State/Prov. _____ Zip/Postal Code _____

Signature (if under 18, a parent or guardian must sign) _____

Mail to the **Harlequin® Reader Service:**
IN U.S.A.: P.O. Box 1867, Buffalo, NY 14240-1867
IN CANADA: P.O. Box 609, Fort Erie, Ontario L2A 5X3

Want to try two free books from another line?
Call 1-800-873-8635 or visit www.ReaderService.com.

* Terms and prices subject to change without notice. Prices do not include applicable taxes. Sales tax applicable in N.Y. Canadian residents will be charged applicable taxes. Offer not valid in Quebec. This offer is limited to one order per household. Not valid for current subscribers to Harlequin American Romance books. All orders subject to credit approval. Credit or debit balances in a customer's account(s) may be offset by any other outstanding balance owed by or to the customer. Please allow 4 to 6 weeks for delivery. Offer available while quantities last.

Your Privacy—The Harlequin® Reader Service is committed to protecting your privacy. Our Privacy Policy is available online at www.ReaderService.com or upon request from the Harlequin Reader Service.

We make a portion of our mailing list available to reputable third parties that offer products we believe may interest you. If you prefer that we not exchange your name with third parties, or if you wish to clarify or modify your communication preferences, please visit us at www.ReaderService.com/consumerschoice or write to us at Harlequin Reader Service Preference Service, P.O. Box 9062, Buffalo, NY 14269. Include your complete name and address.

HAR13R

This was what Eve wanted, too. Even if she would have preferred not to admit it. Before she could stop herself, before she could think of all the reasons why not, she let Derek pull her closer still. His head dipped. Her breath caught, and her eyes closed. And then all was lost in the first luscious feeling of his lips lightly pressed against hers.

It was a cautious kiss. A gentle kiss that didn't stay gallant for long. At her first quiver of sensation, he flattened his hands over her spine and deepened the kiss, seducing her with the heat of his mouth and the sheer masculinity of his tall, strong body. Yearning swept through her in great enervating waves. Unable to help herself, Eve went up on tiptoe, leaning into his embrace. Throwing caution to the wind, she wreathed her arms about his neck and kissed him back. Not tentatively, not sweetly, but with all the hunger and need she felt. And to her wonder and delight, he kissed her back in kind, again and again and again.

Derek had only meant to show Eve they had chemistry. Amazing chemistry that would convince her to go out with him, at least once. He hadn't expected to feel tenderness well inside him, even as his body went hard with desire. He hadn't expected to want to make love to her here and now, in this empty house. But sensing that total surrender would be a mistake, he tamped down his own desire and let the kiss come to a slow, gradual end.

Eve stepped backward, too, a mixture of surprise and pleasure on her face. Her breasts were rising and falling quickly, and her lips were moist. Amazement at the potency of their attraction, and something else a lot more cautious, appeared in her eyes. Eve drew a breath, and then anger flashed. "That was a mistake."

Derek understood her need to play down what had just happened, even as he saw no reason to pretend they hadn't enjoyed themselves immensely. "Not in my book," he murmured, still feeling a little off balance himself. In fact, he was ready for a whole lot more.

Can Derek convince Eve to take a chance
on him this Christmas?

Find out in
THE TEXAS CHRISTMAS GIFT
by Cathy Gillen Thacker
Available December 3, only from
Harlequin® American Romance®.

American Romance®

Since the first grade, Holly Johnson has known that Ramon Rodriguez is the only man for her. But the carefree, determinedly single Texas cowboy with the killer smile doesn't have a clue. Until they share a dance and a kiss… and Ray finally sees his best friend for the woman in love she is. Now that he realizes what he's been missing, Ray plans to make up for lost time…starting with the three little words Holly's waited thirteen years to hear.

The Cowboy's Christmas Surprise
by *USA TODAY* bestselling author
MARIE FERRARELLA

**Available November 5,
from Harlequin® American Romance®.**

HAR75482